RESILIENT

RESILIENT

A (Web-Based Episodic) Musical Play & Story

A Lord Baldwin Happening

'RESILIENT'

A (WEB-BASED EPISODIC)

MUSICAL PLAY & STORY

ACT ONE

Screenplay:
LORD CHESTER L. BALDWIN II

Music
LORD BALDWIN

Lyrics
LORD BALDWIN
(LORD CHESTER L. BALDWIN II)

Except: "Are You Really My Friend"

Lyrics
Tabby (Ruby) Bastion Baldwin & Lord Baldwin

Editing & Suggestions
Meridith Anne Baldwin
&
Elizabeth Baldwin

— AUTHOR'S NOTES —

— AUTHOR'S NOTES —

Okay, so when I set out to write a musical I had no idea how to go about it. Obviously I had a bit of a handle on the music song and dance thing,... I do write poetry for lyrics and I do compose music to accompany the words so as to create songs,... but everything is conceptual in my head,... I'm not able to write the musical compositions like my good friend Mark, who also composes his own piano pieces,... but I do have something in there that cries out to be discovered, and recognized,... and after all, there are many sides to the process, the larger amount in my opinion is what is said in the lyrics (poetry) to drive the narrative and actions of the story to move it forward.

As far as the playwrighting end of it,... well, I looked up its formatting process on the internet and tried following a basic set-up presentation where;... the Act and Scene headings are centered and the character's names are centered and capitalized,... the character's names in stage directions are capitalized,...there are stage directions, indented one tab and then italicized,... and parenthetical stage directions,... and in keeping with the basic elements of a play script;... first, the name of the play and the playwright,... second; Acts and Scenes where each scene described the setting at the start,... third; developed my characters, (maybe a bit too much),...

fourth; maintain good dialogues, and fifth, giving stage directions for the actors/actresses.

So, I set out to write this play,... and it was awkward, clumsy at times, and from an artistic perspective, I found the process using the afore mentioned formatting processes to be unpleasant, obnoxious and frankly, from an artistic perspective, unattractive,... but I persisted to that end, and when I was done, I printed out the play, and put it in a manila envelope along with the CD of the music and words and delivered the package to my friend James, of whom I'd been friends with for over thirty years; he was a guy that had devoted his entire life to the theatre,... I delivered the package to James with hopes that he would read the script and listen to the music and call me up that same day and say, 'Wow, Chester,... you've got something special here." But as I was driving home, I realized how much of an imposition it was for James to have yet another wannabe playwright, dump their work onto him,... playwrights with expectations of receiving flowery if not complimentary comments and maybe,... maybe this would be the one to knock James' socks off and he would say the play was wonderful,... but deep in my heart I kind a knew that, 'RESILIENT' was not really that special,... it had no hauntingly memorable music and words like Rogers and Hammerstein,... I knew the formatting was off a bit but I thought that may be forgiven,... but that he would say the play was something of a long shot,...

And, reality check,... things did not go so well,... James called me up not more than a week or so later, asking me to pick the play back up,... As I stood at James' doorway and he opened his door, there was a sudden chill in the late summer air as James handed me the manila envelope and said something to the effect that the play was hard to read and it seemed to him that it read more like a movie script than a play,... (is that so bad?),... and he mentioned that with 19 songs being over an hour and a half in and of itself,... and with the dialog, (which he felt was too wordy) was way too long for a normal play, and I was told that the general rule of thumb is that a screenplay written in the proper format is equivalent to one page per minute of screen time. Therefore, a screenplay for a two-hour movie will be 120 pages, (2 hours = 120 minutes = 120 pages),... and from James' analogy, this play with too many pages of dialog and 19 musical presentations, would be well over four hours long,... and after thrusting the package back into my hands, James politely wished me well and literally shut the door to his apartment, leaving me standing on his doorstep wondering what just happened,... Yes, it was an awkward moment and I realized once again I had fallen short of my expectations and worse, I'd overstepped my welcome by inconveniencing my friendship by obligating James to the task,... and in James' defense, he was kind enough to scratch down some notes of observations on a few of the front pages,... helpful criticisms and suggestions which I appreciated,... but I knew that I'd unwittingly burned a bridge of friendship that we had had, and that saddened me,...

The manila envelope sat gathering dust in my bedroom for months until, at my daughter Meridith's request, I passed the script and music package to her just before she returned to California,... Meridith, along with Liz, have degrees in theatre from Western

Washington University and the both of them have scads of experience in all facets of the theatre's workings,...

And it was Meridith that came up with the genius idea that if I was to make this play an episodic, web-based production, it wouldn't matter how long the play was as each episode could be as long or as short as each scene or combination of scenes and songs,... And if I was to break things down into eight episodes, give or take each episode to be a half hour long, I could make this thing work.

So I decided to work over the script even more, changed the formatting a bit for easier reading while maintaining some expected formatting,... and, instead of worrying about the musical content, I decided to concentrate on and make a book about the story end of the play and let the reader decide if they even want to hear the music to the songs included in the play,... and for the reader, if so desired, could never mind about the possible connections one can make with the extemporaneous musical numbers,... hopefully it's a good story told about nine individuals going through a hard time as they're getting evicted from their homes within a tent encampment,...

And after that being said, this might be a good starting place for me to jump into some particulars;... I published the, 'RESILIENT' album before I finished the play,... the album consisted of 18 pieces, 16 songs and two musical compositions,...

ACT ONE consisting of intro music, (*Trouble*) followed by seven numbers; *On Your Way To Pismo Beach, Struggling To Get Back, On*

The Cover Of The AARP, Bobcat Ridge (Revisited) , Are You Really My Friend, She Takes Care Of Me, Mr. Lazy Bones,...

ACT TWO consisting of intro music, (*Planet Z*) followed by eight numbers; *My Best Friend, Looking Like The Enemy, I'll Make A Space For You, Fading Away, Ya Gotta Move On, Sending Out A Message, When Love Doesn't Take Off*, and *RESILIENT (Rise And Shine,...*

As I shared with you earlier, I published the, 'RESILIENT' album before I finished the play and things went well until I got to the ending which seemed to me to be rather empty,... and it wasn't just the strong sense of hopelessness to the end of the story, but I didn't want to change things just because it carried a certain sense of hopelessness, after all, the story's backdrop is about the expulsion,... and the story wouldn't feel complete if the ending was unbelievable,... and the way it was, we would be involved with a mother-daughter shared song about, '*When Love Doesn't Take Off*,' followed by the finale piece, '*RESILIENT (Rise And Shine)*,' but to me it seemed like it was missing something,...

So from the play's mood perspective I wrote some dialog between Hoot and Faith, which, drew them closer to each other and brought a small sense of hope to the ending of the story,... then I thought that maybe the dialog might better be served with a poetic notation and then that transitioned it into a musical number,... and with the addition of Hoot and Faith singing, '*What We've Done With Our Lives*' to the story, the momentum of the end of the play shifted to have the reader feel Hoot and Faith's hopefulness for the future,... and the whole of the story seemed to come together,...

For you, the listener, there is a small problem with this alteration, that is, to listen to, '*What We've Done With Our Lives,*' you'll have to go the next album, '*When The World Opens Up Again*' to hear, '*What We've Done With Our Lives.*' I know this is a slight inconvenience, and I may publish a new album to reflect its inclusion, but for now, this is what you get,...

One morning in the fall of 2018 as I was volunteering at the Community Care Center, (CCC), a young man about thirty five came in carrying a backpack and an old, beater guitar with a frayed rope for a strap tied to the guitar that was strapped across his shoulder,... He was checking on his paperwork that he had submitted weeks earlier,... and while he was waiting for a chance to speak with a navigator, (a person that works for Sidewalk interacting with our guests to complete the paperwork and determine eligibility'), he began to nonchalantly talk about his problems,... like, '*losing his job when they found out he'd recently been released from the county jail*' and then, "*he told me he was hungry but his chance for breakfast had come and gone,*' and he told me that, '*he'd be sleeping tonight under the 4th Avenue bridge,*' and he was a bit miffed when he told me, '*all of my stuff got stolen out of my friend's tent,*' and finally, after looking around the room at the other, 'guests' before saying something to the fact that, *everyone at the CCC is in survival mode*,... Meanwhile I knew a golden opportunity when I hear one and with his consent, I was sitting across from him, jotting down notes as fast as I could. The clincher to this story was when I gave him a set of heavy duty boot laces to replace his fractured rope, he pulled his beater guitar off his shoulder and I could see that he had written, "**Struggling**' on the front facing of the guitar with a permeant black marker,...

After he left, I literally wrote the poem (lyrics) to the song, '*Struggling To Get Back*' in about a half an hour while sitting there waiting for our next, 'client',... and I wasted no time that night, creating a tune and then literally recorded all the tracks to the song,...

The following week I went downtown to a local shop called, 'Traditions Café' where the owners did open mike sessions for artists with original material on the first Tuesdays of the month, and of course, I played that song,... it was well received, and I knew I had created something relevant to the times,... and I knew the direction I was to take the next album, 'RESILIENT,'... and although the idea of doing my first musical play was still in the back of my mind I knew it had to come to be,... and I hope you ,the reader, may enjoy this story and that you, the lover of musical plays, can enjoy the music and poetry, (lyrics),... and for you, James,... please accept my apologies for my imposition on our friendship,... please accept this story book as a token of my hopes to mend that bridge,...

I

CAST OF CHARACTERS

CAST

OF

CHARACTERS

2

GLADSTONE

GLADSTONE

A FREE SPIRIT THAT IS FULL OF QUIET KINDNESS. His positive attitude and excitement for simple things sometimes annoys some folks in his homeless community, but most are drawn to, and indeed, fed by his continued sense of optimistic hope. He is not a thin man but not overweight either.

He is an avid comic book reader and has a small but impressive collection in his tent. He is a cartoonologist, with preferences to older animations from the 30s by Max Fleischer and Disney and loves the 40s Warner Brothers material. Gladstone always has a harmonica in one of his pockets.

He secretly calls himself *the Protector* and believes himself to be a kind of comic book hero. As *the Protector* he goes out each night, looking over his sector or subdivision of downtown, keeping the streets safe for the weak and helpless. Because he possesses no super powers, sometimes he gets himself into trouble and sometimes he gets hurt. He lost his job as a salesman for a large telemarketing company after his boss, an aggressive woman that wanted all her salespersons to be as aggressive as she was, pitted all the salespeople up against each other, and Gladstone ended too many times at the bottom of the competition. Gladstone was able to stay in his apartment, living on unemployment and food stamps along what meager money he had saved up. This continued until his landlord raised his rent by 50 dollars a month. He has been homeless for six months.

GLADSTONE SONGS:

On Your Way To Pismo Beach
I'll Make A Space For You
Resilient (Rise And Shine) (Finale)

3

PRIVATE

PRIVATE

A VIETNAM WAR VETERAN, where, for the first six years after returning home from the war, Private was disturbed by ongoing bouts of posttraumatic stress disorder. After a while, the PTSD seemed to level off. A few years later he began having other health issues like, blurred vision, hearing problems, a nervous system condition that causes numbness, tingling, and muscle weakness.

The Veterans Administration has rated his disabling condition to be less than it truly is so instead of getting needed treatment, he is living on medication to help him deal with his pain. Although he is digressing with his illnesses, he finds it hard to get in to see someone at the VA medical facility where he is not evaluated honestly.

Private's nervous system problems worsened, which eventually caused him to down grade his job responsibilities, until the work became too physically and mentally difficult and he became unemployable. Still, his compensation and pension were enough for him to sustain affordable housing, until his rental costs became too high and he was eventually evicted.

When Private became homeless he took up residence living a tent encampment downtown, called "Selbyville," named after the mayor. Private's tent is located inside Selbyville in a small, separated portion of tents called the Circle, named because of the positioning of the tents, semi-closed off from the rest of Selbyville with the tents closely placed in a semicircle.

Not long after Private's arrival to the Circle, a large, but well-mannered street dog he calls Dumpster adopted Private and now, Dumpster goes everywhere with him.

Being in constant pain, Private finds moving around is a good distraction and he sometimes spends days away from his tent and the Circle. In spite of his troubles, he remains optimistic and trusting to his circle of friends. He continues to fight the system.

PRIVATE SONGS:

Struggling To Get Back
Bobcat Ridge
Resilient (Rise And Shine) (Finale)

4

HOOT

HOOT

A SINGER/SONGWRITER/PERFORMER, still waiting and has been waiting all his life to be recognized for his musical abilities. He plays guitar, keyboards, harmonica and a sundry of other instruments to grace his recordings. He spends a lot of his free time honing his many songs so when he is finally discovered, he'll be ready. Unfortunately, (and Hoot is well aware of this), he is old now, and aside from a passing performance here and there where he presents small shows, or plays at some open-mike forum, there is far too little interest in the little world of his esoteric "Jazz" singing. Yet he plods on, continuing his poetic writings with fading hopes to someday be validated for his life's efforts. Hoot shares his tent and everything in his life with his lovely wife and best friend, Faith. They have been married over 40 years. To this day Hoot and his wife Faith are not really clear how they lost their home. One day they were contacted by the Bank of America Legal Department's lawyers telling them there was a discrepancy with their mortgage papers. Three months later, they found themselves evicted from their own home. After securing all their household possessions into a storage unit, they moved all their financial holdings out of BOA and into a local credit union. They are slowly saving up their money in hopes of buying another house. Till then, he and Faith are one of the lucky ones to be sanctioned to be able to move into the new mitigation site.

HOOT SONGS:

On The Cover Of The AARP
She Takes Care Of Me
Fading Away
What We've Done With Our Lives
Resilient (Rise And Shine) (Finale)

5

JEROME

JEROME

A MAN THAT BELIEVES HIMSELF TO BE HIGHLY INTEL-LIGENT, and he believes that he is tuned in and aware of things around him; political, scientific and metaphysical things that others are not. He is suspicious of everyone until he gets to know them and even then, he is reluctant to let certain people in his sphere. It would seem at times that he is wearing the mantle of homelessness to hide out from his enemies and his past. Being a deep-seated conspiracy theorist, Jerome believes in a lot of wild ideas and notions as to what is going on in the world. Thinking himself to be one of the chosen few, he speaks with a note of expertise, even though to others his statements may sound outrageous. He is dubious of authority, like the government or the police and he is always vigilantly watching his back; always looking around to see who's there. Jerome was raised in foster homes, was kicked out of high school at sixteen and when he turned eighteen, the system released him out into the world. He still believes it was part of some nefarious scheme to get him to reveal his true self. He is especially fearful that the government is watching him; either waiting for their opportunity to bring him in for questioning to find out what he knows or to abduct him to bring to one of their secret installations and run experiments on him.

JEROME SONGS:

They're Taking Over
You Gotta Move On
Resilient (Rise And Shine) (Finale)

6

ANGEL

ANGEL

A TEENAGE GIRL LIVING WITH AND MOSTLY TAKING CARE OF HER MOTHER, Scrounge. In spite her having learning disabilities and challenges and having trouble staying focused for any length of time, she is an accomplished artist both with regular mediums like pencil/pen as well as digital art using computer and her phone and can create art for hours. Because she has no permanent address, she goes to an alternative high school off and on, depending on favorable circumstances and whether or not she feels she can leave her mother alone for a while. When at school, Angel loves the physical and interpretive dance classes. Even though she is not very good, she aspires to be a dancer, and understands that she is still in the beginning stages of training or direction. When Angel was young, her grandparents offered her and her mother a place to stay to get off the streets, and Angel would have loved to be with her grandparents and to live in more stable circumstances, but her mother does not.

ANGEL SONGS:

Are You Really My Friend?
When Love Doesn't Take Off
Resilient (Rise And Shine) (Finale)

7

FAITH

FAITH

A GENTLE, THOUGHTFUL AND GENEROUS WOMAN, full of kindness, compassion and good will. Being charitable to a fault, and a good listener she is visited often by many of the women (and men) in the camp who come to her for advice and to talk about their circumstances. Faith has a good heart and people around her know that she might not have answers to their problems, but she has a genuine empathy for these folks in their temporary state of non-existence; where the laws and the system seem to nullify their worth. And even when others in this tent community can be indifferent or unsympathetic to another's plight, most folks know that Faith will take the time to genuinely listen; and they know she cares.

Faith's empathic nature does bother Hoot at times because most of the homeless have little regard to her needs, time or the apparent imposition they take advantage of, or the bothersome nuisance they become as they call at all hours of the day and night. But Hoot tolerates it most of the time because he knows the ministering that his wife does is important.

Besides being an enigmatologist, especially with crossword puzzles, Faith is an avid genealogist in search of living and deceased family members, for both her and Hoot. Using a laptop and her cell phone, she takes every free opportunity she has to search for relatives; this is of course when she has a Wi-Fi connection which can be got at the local libraries, the Union Gospel Mission and the day room at the Community Care Center. She has also helped a few of the older/interested folks in their camp with learning how they can search for their own relatives. Faith has a quiet but strong spiritual conscientious that is felt by all around her. This special spirit or light can sometimes illuminate a good influence on otherwise misguided individuals. Faith and her husband Hoot, with their optimistic perspectives, may seem strangely out of place, but they are loved.

FAITH SONGS:

My Best Friend
Sending Out A Message
What We've Done With Our Lives
Resilient (Rise And Shine) (Finale)

8

BOBBY

BOBBY

WHEN BOBBY WAS TWO, her parents crossed over from Mexico into Arizona and then moved to Fresno California where her father's brother and his family lived. Bobby played Saxophone in her High School marching band. Things were fine until the U.S. Immigration and Customs Enforcement (ICE) started cracking down on undocumented immigrants and grabbed her father and two of her cousins and deported them back to Mexico. Bobby and her mother narrowly escaped and drove a borrowed vehicle to Las Vegas and then, with a number of buses, took a crisscross route to end up in Yakama, Washington where they stayed with shirttail relatives.

Bobby is a female boxer, boxing in short bouts, comprising four rounds of two minutes, each with a one-minute interval between rounds as a featherweight in the 119-pound amateur weight division. For her it is a physical game of chess, all about outscoring and outclassing her opponent. She has won many consecutive matches and was on a fast track to becoming Professional until she found out that pro boxing, especially for women, was not cost effective. Staying amateur made her happy even though she got moved around and used; boxing out of her class and sometimes forced to box out of her weight division.

As part of the president's nationwide crackdown, the ICE showed up in Yakama and started rounding up anyone that looked Latino. One day she was leaving the Athletic Club's training center and she became aware that she was being followed. After they tried to stop her, she ran into the Tahoma Cemetery and was able to ditch them. She hid out under a bridge spanning the Naches River overnight and then hitchhiked down backroads through Packwood and Morton till she got to Olympia.

Although she lives in constant fear of being taken away, and although she is in hiding, every day she remains in constant training and stays in shape by running 3 to 5 miles, jumping ropes for 30 minutes and she has an army duffle bag that is stuffed full of old clothes and mounted vertically with wooden pallets, that she punches and spars with for 30 minutes every day. She remains hopeful she'll be able to box again.

BOBBY SONGS:

Looking Like The Enemy
Resilient (Rise And Shine) (Finale)

9

PRINCESS

PRINCESS

PRINCESS IS THE OLDEST OF FOUR SIBLINGS, was raised in a two-income household that struggled to meet their financial needs. Around the time that Princess was ten her teacher at school began noticing that Princess was having trouble in class. She had difficulty concentrating and was having relationship problems with classmates who could not relate with her sudden feelings of sadness and her notions of overwhelming fear for no reason or feelings of helplessness, anger and frustration. When she suddenly had changes in her personality; intense enough to interfere with her daily activities, the school stepped in. She was evaluated by a school therapist who recommended she get further studies, but the financial implications for these medical procedures scared Princess's mother and Princess was withdrawn from school. This left Princess alone at home, where she would hear voices of people that weren't there. This fostered a questioning of ideas in her mind about the reality of things, and at times, even who she was. The only person that connected with Princess was her brother Dan who seemed to understand her and even guided her back to a comfortable version of one of her realities when she stepped too far away. Not long after, her father, not wanting to deal with his troublesome wife and broken daughter, left, leaving the strain of raising a child with mental disorders and three other children, squarely on her mother; a woman working full time, with little understanding but even less tolerance for dealing with a broken girl. As her monetary circumstances declined, Princess's mother reluctantly had to rely on the state for financial assistance. When the state offered free treatment for Princess, her mother was agreeable. After psychotherapy, followed by varied medications, which seemed to make matters worse, Princess's mother was happy to have her daughter institutionalized, especially when she found it would be free. Over a year ago the behavioral health doctors found unmistakable improvements with Princess and her condition, and she was let out with an arrangement that she would be reevaluated every three months. On her return to her family, her brother Dan helped Princess to get a job and even let her borrow one of his cars. But Princess was not well received by her mother who had thought that she was done dealing with Princess. Tensions between her and her mother escalated so badly that Princess left and never returned. And she never went back to be reevaluated either.

PRINCESS SONGS:

Resilient (Rise And Shine) (Finale)

10

SCROUNGE

SCROUNGE

A RATHER YOUNGER WOMAN THAT LOOKS DECID-
EDLY OLDER THAN SHE IS. She dropped out of high school, ran
away from her home in Cle Elum Washington to move to Seattle.
Knowing herself to have a keen eye and impeccable taste, she hoped
to be an art director working in advertising, magazine publishing
or especially, Television production. But without even a basic edu-
cation she was lucky to get a job at a fast food restaurant, making
just enough to pay the rent and her monthly bills.

Meanwhile, in her spare time she would visit advertising agen-
cies and television/network offices trying to get hired and hopefully work her way up the corporate ladder. Unfortunately, because
Scrounge found it painful to expend effort on any long-term goals
that did not provide instant gratification, she would only embark
on what she felt was worthwhile projects. She had a hard time
factoring in the longer-term benefits or consequences and would

tend to distrust and discount a return that was distant or uncertain. Scrounge would only continue in a certain direction if she believed that the return on her labor would exceed her loss of comfort.

Eventually she did get hired at a small studio where she set up equipment and props for a magazine photographer, but after working for three years with no promotions, she quit, only to find she was pregnant with Angel. Scrounge's parents offered to have her and Angel move back to Cle Elum and help them get back on their feet, but this offer annoyed Scrounge and she would have nothing to do with it.

Instead, Scrounge became dependent on the State where she could obtain and accept money, food stamps and other benefits from the system for her needs, without doing or intending to do anything in return. But Scrounge lost her benefits because of fraudulent claims. Scrounge gravitated to a tent community where living was less complicated and she could still sponge off the local community's offerings as well as everyone around her.

At times Scrounge would like to blame her sad situation on her daughter, Angel, but after years of dealing with the inflicted guilt, Angel realized what was happening and went into a state of ignoring her mother. Scrounge has come to know that her daughter loves her and continues to take care of her, but otherwise, because Scrounge is so preoccupied with her circumstances, she is ignorant to her daughter's needs.

Scrounge talks about wanting to make a triumphant return to the public sector and become an art director, and leave her homelessness behind, but she has no concrete plans on how to do that.

She has become an expert scrounge and scavenge, harboring many gray areas between foraging, finding, borrowing and stealing.

SCROUNGE SONGS:

Mr. Lazy Bones
When Love Doesn't Take Off
Resilient (Rise And Shine) (Finale)

II

List of Music and Songs for ACT ONE

LIST OF MUSIC AND SONGS FOR ACT ONE

Trouble

PRELUDE MUSIC   ACT ONE, SCENE ONE

On Your Way To Pismo Beach

GLADSTONE *   ACT ONE, SCENE FOUR

Struggling To Get Back

PRIVATE *   ACT ONE, SCENE FIVE

On The Cover Of The AARP

HOOT *   ACT ONE, SCENE EIGHT

Bobcat Ridge (Revisited)

PRIVATE *   ACT ONE, SCENE NINE

They're Taking Over

JEROME *   ACT ONE, SCENE TEN

Are You Really My Friend

ANGEL *   ACT ONE, SCENE TWELVE

She Takes Care Of Me

HOOT *   ACT ONE, SCENE THIRTEEN

Mr. Lazy Bones

SCROUNGE *   ACT ONE, SCENE FOURTEEN

LIST OF MUSIC AND SONGS
AND THE PERFORMERS
FOR ACT TWO

Planet Z

INTERLUDE MUSIC   ACT TWO, SCENE ONE

My Best Friend

FAITH *   ACT TWO, SCENE THREE

Looking Like The Enemy

BOBBY *   ACT TWO, SCENE FOUR

I'll Make A Space For You

GLADSTONE *   ACT TWO, SCENE FIVE

Fading Away

HOOT *   ACT TWO, SCENE SIX

Ya Gotta Move On

JEROME *   ACT TWO, SCENE EIGHT

Sending Out A Message

FAITH *   ACT TWO, SCENE NINE

When Love Doesn't Take Off

ANGEL & SCROUNGE * ACT TWO, SCENE TEN

What We've Done With Our Lives

HOOT & FAITH *   ACT TWO, SCENE ELEVEN

"RESILIENT"

EVERYONE (in parts)   ACT TWO, SCENE TWELVE

I2

ACT ONE - SCENE ONE

ACT ONE — SCENE ONE: ("A")

The Players:
GLADSTONE & PRINCESS

(This scene is how I originally envisioned the beginning of the play – unfortunately it would require a scene change afterwards to get to scene two) *

EMPTY STAGE LIT WITH DARK BLUE LIGHTS TO EXEM-PLIFY NIGHT - As the prelude music, "Trouble" begins, a person or persons come on the stage and in the darkness, they set up a tent. This is followed by a second and third and fourth and so on till ten tents are assembled. As the people come on the stage, they are humming or singing softly, one of the three main themes from "Trouble" as they set up their tents. *

NOTE: The Prelude music, "Trouble" is three minutes and

twenty-three seconds long, do the stage setting must be done in that timeframe. *

ACT ONE — SCENE ONE: ("B")

The Players:
GLADSTONE & PRINCESS

(This coincides more fluently with Scene two)

EXT. TIMEWORN BRICK SALVATION ARMY BUILDING – MORNING: The unimposing, rather rundown building has faulty brickwork in places sadly in need of repair, *

The prelude music, "Trouble" is playing in the background as people are coming, one or two at a time, humming or singing softly, one of the three main themes from "Trouble" as they get in a make-shift line, waiting for the doors to open in the basement of the Salvation Army. *

There is a cold early March breeze that scatters debris past their feet and the biting cold causes the people to huddle and shiver as they wait in line. *

13

❦

(An ACT ONE - SCENE ONE Possibility)

(ANOTHER SCREENPLAY POSSIBILITY)

The Players:
GLADSTONE & PRINCESS

SALVATION ARMY BUILDING. Unimposing, rather rundown and brickwork in need of repair, *

The prelude music, "Trouble" is playing in the background as people are coming, one or two at a time, humming or singing softly, one of the three main themes from "Trouble" as they get in a make-shift line, waiting for the doors to open to the basement of the Salvation Army kitchen and cafeteria. There is a cold early March breeze that scatters debris past their feet and the biting cold causes the people to huddle and shiver as they wait in line. *

NARRATOR (V.O.)

"Once upon a time on the very streets of your city, a fair young Princess was living in her car,..." *

RACK FOCUS to fogged up windows of an older Ford Focus car. *

NARRATOR (V.O.)

"It is a typical gray, rainy morning as the young Princess pops her head out from under an inadequate blanket to look at her watch." *

NARRATOR (V.O.)

"Although she had seemingly fallen on rather hard times, the Princess remained hopeful, noble and kind." *

ACT ONE — SCENE TWO

ACT ONE — SCENE TWO:

The Players:
GLADSTONE & PRINCESS

INT. SALVATION ARMY BASEMENT DINING ROOM - MORNING: It's just a little after 7:00 AM. People are in a line to get breakfast at 7:15 AM. As people find seats in the dining area, they are unconscientiously looking down into their food, humming to one of the three themes to the tune, "Trouble" that is softly playing in the background *

At a fold-out table sits Gladstone; a young man with eyes filled with optimistic hope. He is wearing a Kelly-green suit, brownish green spats over Beatle boots, a flamboyant paisley bow-tie and a wide-brimmed fedora of which he has many,... today it is super-man blue.

Gladstone, sporting a Tony Stark moustache, was early to the Salvation Army facility and close to the front of the line and so, was one of the first people to get food. *

A young woman steps into the doorway and glances at a sign that reads, "Please sign in to use the community kitchen." *

A lady behind the counter serving food sees the anxiety on the young woman's face and says, "You don't have to give anything but your first name, love." *

The young woman smiles nervously as she writes, "Princess M." and takes her place in line. When she gets her tray, she walks over to a fold-out table and sits across from Gladstone. *

"Saw you sleeping in your car." Gladstone says without looking up, forking food in his mouth. *

"Really?" Princess replies with concern. "And who are you?" *

Gladstone stops eating. His lips quiver for a few seconds before he looks up to answer. He is suddenly thrown off guard as he looks into and discovers her beautiful blue eyes. "Gladstone." He answers, turning his attention back to his food.
"And that wasn't a very good street to park your car on." He says flinching. He looks up again and smiles as he says, "I'm glad you made it here okay though." *

"Thank you." Princess says with a note of derision in her voice *

"It was the fourth night." Gladstone said, looking down again, stirring his eggs with a fork.*

In the background, the humming of "Trouble" in four-part harmony seems to get louder. *

"You've been counting how many nights I sleep in my car?" Princess barks, rather annoyed. "I don't know who you are,..." She says as she moves to stand up. *

"Hey," Gladstone says with a note of seriousness, putting down his fork as he looks over at her again. "Please, wait a second." Gladstone says moving himself backwards to appear less threatening. "I ain't no stalker. But they are out there." He grimaces. "I'm just saying, you need to be careful." *

Princess, with mixture of confusion and curiosity, stares back at Gladstone as she sits back down. Sensing care and honesty in Gladstone's face, she says, "My name is Princess. And I'm sorry, I, I didn't mean,..." *

"It's okay." Gladstone says, raising his hands up in surrender and smiles again before asking, "Princess M, eh. That wouldn't be for Princess Mononoke would it?" *

"I'm not sure what you're talking about,..." Princess says with a note of confusion. *

"It's a Hayao Miyazaki animation,... 1997,..." Gladstone answers, looking down at the table. "But never mind that." He says looking up. "So why today?" He says with furrowed brows. "I mean, this is the first time you decided to come in. Didn't you get hungry?" *

"More than you know." Princess replies, looking at her food, "I had a hard time deciding." *

"You couldn't decide whether you were hungry or not?" Gladstone asks. *

"Well," Princess replies dubiously, "I couldn't get up the courage to come in." *

Gladstone nods understandingly and says, "I got ya. Well, I know it's never easy." *

"I got evicted Thursday." Princess interjects, looking down, embarrassed. *

"Hey," Gladstone says, looking thoughtfully around the room. "Lot a that going round." *

"Well I'm glad I finally got the nerve to come in here." Princess says optimistically. *

"Look, I don't know your circumstances," Gladstone says, blinking his eyes irregularly, "but it'd be safer for you to just find a better place to stay."

"Have you thought about calling up your folks and letting them know how things are for you right now?" *

Princess hesitates before answering, "That's not an option for me right now." *

"Yeah, okay,…" Gladstone replies, "Me neither. That's why I'm living in a tent." *

"Living in a tent?" Princess asks with a curious look on her face. *

"Yeah," Gladstone answers, "Right next to the bus transit center, you know, on State Street?" *

No, not sure," Princess replies, "but about moving my car to somewhere else?" *

"Yeah?" Gladstone replies. "I can give you a few recommendations where to park overnight in this city." *

"That'd be nice." Princess replies softly before shoveling a huge amount
of scrambled eggs and toast with hamburger gravy into her mouth. *

Gladstone stands, reaches into his coat and pulls out a map and says, "Let's see here,…" Seeing Gladstone so prepared with a map, Princess laughs. She and Gladstone survey the map. *

15

ACT ONE - SCENE THREE

ACT ONE — SCENE THREE:

The Players:
GLADSTONE & PRINCESS

EXT. SIDEWALK, CITY STREETS: Princess and Gladstone are talking and walking on their way to move Princess'S car. They turn a corner, a block away from her car, Princess looks down the street, stops abruptly and suddenly turns around and quickly runs back, out of sight.*

Gladstone follows her and when they're both out of sight he asks, "What's the matter?" *

"They found me." Princess answers, her eyes wild with fear. *

"Who found you?" Gladstone asks, looking back and forth. *

Princess does not answer, but instead says, "Could you go look and see if there's someone over there?" *

"What?' Gladstone questions. *

"They don't know you." She replies. *

"What?" Gladstone asks. "Who are *they*?" *

"I don't know." She answers. *

"You don't know?" Gladstone parrots "What is it I'm supposed to be looking for?" *

"My car two blocks down the street. It's a,..." *

"A Seahawks green Ford Focus," Gladstone interjects, "yeah I know it, but,..." *

"Look;" Princess says with a whispered yell, "I thought I saw some men hovering over my car. Could you please just look and see if there's anybody there?" She pauses and says, "Sometimes I see things that aren't there. You know?" *

Gladstone looks at her for a second before he walks calmly around the corner and gazes down the street where her Ford Focus is parked. He turns his head slightly and says softly behind him, "Yeah; there's two guys in suits; one tall the other medium. They're hanging around and leaning on a white cargo van behind yours, but they don't seem to be in any hurry to go anywhere." Gladstone steps back around the corner to discuss options with Princess, but she is gone. He looks around and seeing no sign of Princess, and decides to walk down the sidewalk to her car. When he gets to the car, he pretends not to notice the two men and he walks over to the driver's side of the Ford and tries to open the door. *

Almost immediately, the two men look at each other before they step up a few feet from Gladstone. The taller of the two asks, "Hey, is this your car?" *

"No." Gladstone answers nonchalantly. "Not yet. But it could be mine,…" He says as he looks back at the two men. "if I end up buying it." *

"What do you mean?" The shorter man asks suspiciously. *

"Hey what's it to ya?" Gladstone asks. "Don't tell me she already sold it to you guys? *

"Sold it?" The shorter man asks. *

"No." The tall man quickly interjects. "How much did she say she was selling it for to you?" *

"Hey." Gladstone says with an annoyed look on his face. "What are you guys doing here?" *

"What?" The tall man asks, glancing at his partner. *

"You're crowding me, man." Gladstone says waving his hands as if to say, give me some space. After the two men retreat to standing in front of their cargo van again, Gladstone says, "I'm not sure I want to tell you guys,... You'll out bid me."

Gladstone walks to the front of the car, inspecting the front hood and bumper and moving around the car examining all the particulars; tires, doors, then walks past the two men and examines the back trunk. Meanwhile the two men follow his movements with their eyes. *

The tall man finally says, "Hey, you come from the circus or something?" *

"Yeah, the shorter man laughs, "That green suit, bow-tie and a blue hat looks like you're,..." *

"Funny." Gladstone says without looking up at the two men as he reinspects the tires and checks to see if any of the doors are unlocked. *

"Look, we don't want the car. The shorter man says guardedly apologetic. "I'm uh, her brother and I'd just like to get in touch with her, that's all." *

"Oh." Gladstone replies warmly. "And what's your name.?" *

Both men suddenly take on a different demeanor; one of surprise, the other of annoyance and indignation. "We don't want the car." The tall man interjects with a note of impatience in his voice. *

"Oh, sorry." Gladstone postures. "I was afraid you guys heard she was selling the car and,..." *

The shorter man touches the tall man on the shoulder and says, "Sorry, my friend here has had a problem with his car this morning, that's why we're driving this rig. Tell you what, though. I got a friend that's getting transferred overseas and he's selling his Honda Civic, real cheap." The short man smiles and says, "You give me your name and number and I'll pass it along." *

"Hmm, sorry guys,... " Gladstone says apologetically as he quickly looks past the men, through the front windshield into the darkness of the windowless van where all that can be seen is a heavy chain-link fencing behind the driver's seat. Gladstone walks back to the front of the Ford Focus to give him some safe distance from the two men before he smiles and says, "Tell you what,... you know where the Denny's restaurant is on Martin Way?" *

"Yeah?" The Tall man says with a note of uncertainty. *

"I'm supposed to meet up with her there at twelve to buy her lunch and, to seal the deal." *

The shorter man looks at the taller man before turning to Gladstone and says, "Okay, thanks." They both turn to get into the cargo van but the taller man turns around and asks, "By the way, what's your name?" *

"You don't need to see my identification..." Gladstone replies, waving his hand.
"These aren't the droids you're looking for." *

"What?" The taller man asks looking confused. *

The shorter man with a note of annoyance, says to Gladstone, "He asked you,... what's your name?" *

"Hmm,..." Gladstone replies with a knowing smile, "I could ask you both the same question." Gladstone stands, leaning on the front hood of the Ford Focus as the two men get into their van and drive away, but not before he notices that the front license plate is missing and the back plate has a small vertical "XMT" in small letters and the numbers, "14785" and the letter, "C."

Gladstone waits for a few minutes to make sure they don't double back to follow him, and just to be sure, when he does leave, he cuts through a passageway between two houses and then snakes his way through alleys and backyards where he knows he can't be followed. *

16

ACT ONE - SCENE FOUR

ACT ONE — SCENE FOUR:

The Players:
**GLADSTONE, PRINCESS, JEROME, FAITH,
HOOT, ANGEL & SCROUNGE**

EXT. SIDEWALK, CITY STREETS: Gladstone makes his way back to the Salvation Army, checking around inside and out, hoping to meet up with Princess again, but she's not there. He is close to the tent community when he hears a voice calling him from behind. He turns and sees Princess. *

"I saw you a couple blocks back," Princess says, out of breath, "but you're a fast mover." *

Happy to see Princess, Gladstone stops and smiles as she catches up with him. "What happened to you?" Gladstone asks with a curious scowl. "I was worried about you." *

"I kind a freaked out." Princess replies, catching her breath. "So I kind of went down the block from the other side and hid myself and watched from behind the bushes." She stops, causing Gladstone to stop and she asks, "Why did you go down there? I mean, really. Wasn't that dangerous?" *

"Well, you did ask me to go," Gladstone replies, looking curiously at her, "and I thought I was safe." He frowns thoughtfully and says, "They didn't know me and they didn't know if I knew you, and,... one of em told me he was your brother." *

"I was close enough," Princess says astutely, "to see that neither of those guys was my Brother." *

"I didn't think so." Gladstone replies. "He seemed like he was lying. And when he said he was your brother; his friend had a *tell* on his face, like it was news to him." Seeing confusion, Gladstone continues, "A "*tell*" is a slight change in a person's behavior or de-meanor." Gladstone answers. "These guys never rehearsed who they were or why they were there and when the short guy said that he was your brother, the tall guy gave it away; I could see in his eyes that he was surprised." *

"You sound like you're a detective or something." Princess replies with wonder. *

"Used to play poker." Gladstone quips smiling. "But sadly, never good enough to make money with it." He looks at Princess and grimaces before saying, "So what was that *crazy* scene all about?" *

Princess recoils for a moment before answering, "It's kind of a long story,..." She looks back with resignation, "First of all, that is my brother's car." Princess answers Gladstone with a simple air and tone. "He let me borrow it. And how those two figured that out, I don't know." *

"They were fishing, that's all." Gladstone reports. "Do you know either of those guys?" *

"No, never seen em before, but,..." Princess pauses. "But I think they're from Western." *

"Western?" Gladstone parrots. "Western Washington University or Western State Hospital?" *

"I had problems,..." Princess reports as she sits on the sidewalk curb. "with my mind, you know? I was in a place,... the Child Study & Treatment Center till I turned 18 and was transferred to Western. I was there for ,... doesn't matter, but about a year ago I was let out." *

"Well that's not bad." Gladstone returns as he sits next to her. "Doesn't figure though. I mean, why send out the two goons to confront you? Is that how the state works now?" Gladstone sees confusion on Princess's face and says, "That was rhetorical. You're not supposed to have to answer it." *

"I went back to my mother's," Princess continued, now speaking with a note of distant reflection, "and I was scheduled to go back every three months to that place to see how I'm doing, you know, get reevaluated? But my mother couldn't handle me being there in her house. I think she feels guilty for putting me away in the first place, anyway,... so I left." *

"Do you still go to the appointments?" Gladstone asks. *

"No, not really." Princess admits. "And I stopped taking my meds six months ago." *

"But aren't you afraid you'll need the help?" Gladstone asks. "I mean, sometimes medication can help, especially for bi-polar,..." *

"I'm not bi-polar." Princess shouts back defensively, but then says sheepishly, "Least I don't,... She calms herself before saying, "I don't think there was any difference before or after." Princess explains. "Except that before, when I was taking the pills, I was getting these terrible headaches all the time. I don't get em anymore." *

"Hmm." Says Gladstone, scratching the back of his head and squinting. "Sounds a bit of a gamble." *

"You let me worry about that." Princess says unassumingly as she and Gladstone walk down the sidewalk to the mitigation site where there is a sea of tents crammed together in different sizes and configurations. *

Gladstone points across the street to a building and says, "That's the Community Care Center; we call it the, 'CCC' and it's a place where people go during the day to get out of the weather." *

"Nice that it's so close." Princess replies looking over with mild interest. *

Gladstone leads Princess into the encampment to an area where there is a small cluster of tents purposely formed into a semicircle.

He points over at a group of people huddled around an ineffective propane heater, talking to themselves and Gladstone says reports. "There it is; this Circle of Tents, we just call, 'the Circle' it's our little neighborhood." *

"Your neighborhood?" *

"Hey." Gladstone say's, slightly waving his hand. *

In sync, everyone in the small group of people stop talking and look over at Gladstone and at Princess who is obviously uncomfortable. *

"Hey," Gladstone says, "You guys missed some serious hamburger S.O.S. and eggs this morning." *

"Missed?" A man wearing two differently colored cardigan sweaters returns. "Not sure I be missing something that has so many unidentified bits and pieces cobbled together into their concoction." *

"Hey, Jerome," Gladstone says, laughingly, "It's just the stuff left over." *

"Yeah," Jerome says, as he pulls up his loose pants and pulls his sweaters down over his jeans only to have his pants slide down again. "But you have no idea how *many* days and what else is in there." *

"No," Gladstone answers, "but it was good, wasn't it, Princess?" *

Princess sees everyone looking to her as she answers, "I was so hungry that I don't think I really tasted it as I was eating it." She smiles and with raised eyebrows, says, "It was hot,..." *

Everyone laughs. *

"Well, it was probably better than,..." An older man in a blue-gray, wide-brimmed 30s fedora begins." *

"You're down to this again, aren't you, Hoot?" An older woman interrupts, smiling at the older man. *

"Faith. I got this." Hoot replies, readjusting his fedora and smiling at Faith. He turns his head to Princess and says' "Sorry, my wife thinks she knows me." *

"And I do." Faith replies, looking away with a wry grin. "Everything from what you like to eat, to the clothes you wear to the songs you write. And I know you as well as you know your guitar over there." She points to a guitar that is sitting in a stand just outside their tent; a 'Guitar with No Strings.' "I think it's safe to say, I know almost everything about you." *

Hoot, who never looks away from Princess, raises an eyebrow and asks, "So, tell us, what's happening with you, kid?" *

"Well,..." Princess shyly replies. "I'm new at this homelessness thing. Only to be compounded by the fact that I can't go back to my car,..." *

"That was really freaky." Gladstone says, glancing nervously over at Princess for a second. *

"City impound?" Hoot asks. *

"The city is famous for doing whatever they want." Jerome adds. "They have the power." *

A teenage girl wearing a black tee shirt with a silkscreened 'Dejando La Galaxia Pt. 1' album printed on it, along with a short, pastel pink plaid skirt, dark gray tights, and orange ballet shoes steps out of a tent and up next to a barefoot woman in shorts and a ragged, oversized navy pea coat. "Jerome here, is a,..." The teenage girl begins, "What's that called, mom?" *

"A conspiracy theorist, Angel." The woman standing next to the girl answers. *

"Oh yeah," Angel returns gleefully, "A conspiracy theorist. He thinks everyone, especially the government is out to get him. And,..." She smiles and says gleefully, "He believes the world is flat." *

"You're still too young to see what's really going on, Angel." Jerome says, annoyed. "Too young and naïve. In the now famous words from the Jimi Hendrix Experience, "As you all know, you just can't believe everything you see and hear, now can you?"" *

"You're just a crazy." Angel replies nonchalantly, "You think everybody's out to get you." *

"It's not just that," Jerome continues, pulling up his pants again. "Someone needs to stand up for social injustices,..." Jerome shifts his eyes to Angel's mother and says, "But, we're running out of time, Scrounge. And you know that. And if you read between the lines,..." *

"What lines we talking about now?" Scrounge interrupts as she

searches for something in the pockets of her pea coat, and after pulling out and examining scraps of paper in both hands, she returns
the papers to the pockets she pulled them out of and says, "the part
where there's no gravity here on earth? Or the world is hollow? Or
how the Bush administration squirreled away billions in gold after
the war in Iraq? Or,..." *

"Come on Scrounge," Jerome interrupts, "You know you believe
in the 18-billion-dollar gold heist." *

"Yeah," Scrounge admits. "That part I do believe, and I believe all
of the floors of the World Trade Center were set up with explosives
by Dick Cheney to orchestrate the buildings floors to collapse like
they did so the Bush administration could steal all the gold,... I
mean, come on,... but a giant protective shell over the earth that
won't allow anything to get out or in our atmosphere? That's crazy
talk,... but you know?" Scrounge says, looking seriously at Princess.
"I kind of believe in flying saucers." *

"Believe what you will to survive, Scrounge," Jerome replies, "but
we're all in this mess together...." *

"And whether you call this thing here fair or not, Jerome,"
Scrounge rebuts, "you gotta know, in the end,..." *

As Scrounge and Jerome continue to argue and their voices trail
off, Princess turns to Hoot and says, "How can you play that guitar
over there if there's no strings on it?" *

"The guitar is warped from extreme weather." Hoot replies. "But,
the really cool thing about it is that it's a magic guitar and I can hear
the chords in my head when I play it." He looks over at Jerome and

continues, "Jerome and Gladstone here are learning how to play it." He smiles at Jerome and then at Gladstone before saying, "And the really groovy thing about it is, it's very forgiving. If I play a chord wrong, which I haven't done in ages, but if I should play a chord wrong, it still plays right. It's is kind of dynamite, right?" *

"Dynamite." Faith parrots. "You'd think after all these years you could find a much more appropriate or descriptive, post-positive adjective." *

"Faith here is a wordologist." Hoot announces. "Among other things." *

Angel turns to Gladstone and says, "I finished those comics you lent me." Angel quickly disappears into her tent and emerges with a handful of comics. "Can I trade you for some new ones?" She hands the comics to Gladstone. "I really liked the Uncle Scrooge and the Betty & Veronica comics the best." *

Gladstone smiles and says, "Yeah, I got some more of each." He goes into his tent and returns with a fresh stack. "Please take real good care of em,..." *

"Like Angel would do anything else." Scrounge interrupts. *

"So, you're a comic collector?" Princess asks smiling. *

"Collector?" Scrounge mimics, "He's possessed!" *

"And it's not just comics." Angel interjects. "He knows every-thing about cartoons too." She looks over at Gladstone and says questioningly, "Gladstone is a Cartoonologist?" *

"Lets just say, Cartoon Specialist,..." Gladstone corrects. "But I do like that moniker; Cartoonologist. I think I'm gonna keep it." *

"He is truly a master." Hoot interjects. "He knows everything about Disney and Warner Brothers cartoons and Disney comics." *

"Yeah," Faith interjects, "His viewpoints and beliefs in life all seem to center around philosophies he's gathered from his comic books and the cartoons he's watched." *

"True that." Scrounge replies. "He's always spouting off weirdness,..." *

"Not weirdness." Gladstone corrects, looking at Faith with a smile, "Philosophies." *

Gladstone stands to the side of the others, smiles as he sings, "*On Your Way To Pismo Beach*"

17

On Your Way To Pismo
Beach

So, Bugs Bunny's going somewhere,
he's just not getting to where he wants to be
And it's gonna take some time if he keeps on taking
a wrong turn at Albuquerque,
but he doesn't seem to be worried,
even when his destination's out of reach,
Out of reach
I kind think he's hip to knowing
life is what happens on your way to Pismo Beach
Yeah, on your way to Pismo Beach
So, Bugs and Daffy are traveling underground,
on their way to, well you know where
When they came up into this cave
with Ali Baba's treasure just sitting there
And even though Daffy is beguiled;

not wanting full shares for each;
full shares for each
Bugs ain't caring much because he knows
that life is what happens on your way to Pismo Beach;
Yeah, on your way to Pismo Beach
What's Up Doc? Bugs casually asks,
calculating what the next move might be
And, of course you know this means war,
is code for, I'm getting back what you took from me
So, Bugs goes from one adventure to the next,
finding himself in situations to get through
But he's got a good sense of himself and his psyche;
he always seems to figure out what it is he's got to do
Yeah, it's hard to best the Bugs Bunny
for he learns what each lesson might teach;
What each lesson might teach
And from opening credits to That's All Folks
he finds that life is what happens
on your way to Pismo Beach;
Yeah, on your way to Pismo Beach

After singing, Gladstone casually picks up Hoot's 'Guitar with No Strings' and plays out the guitar riff on through the end of the song

18

ACT ONE - SCENE FIVE

ACT ONE — SCENE FIVE:

The Players:
JEROME, PRINCESS, SCROUNGE,
GLADSTONE, HOOT, FAITH & PRIVATE

EXT. GROUP STANDING ASIDE THE TENT ENCAMP-MENT CIRCLE: "It's city thinking. Like,... last Tuesday,..." Jerome says to Princess, "there was a town meeting where they were supposed to have a vote on whether we stay or whether we leave, you know what I mean? But they kind a did this slick stuff where they never did vote on the matter, so when everybody left from being there and were out of the town meeting, that's when the city council voted and then the little green goblins came and put pieces of paper on and in our dwellings, telling us we had to leave." *

"So the city give you guys notice?" Princess asks. "There's a lot of homeless,..." *

"I choose to call it houseless; I'm houseless; homelessness is just a sad state of mind and a label that the outside can use to justify their own circumstances; something that they; whoever or whatever they are, can point their fingers at, from a safe distance, as they drive by, and say to their precious; "Now looky there, that's what will happen to you, child, if you don't stay on the right track." *

"I get that," Princess says, "but, I mean, you're kind a being evicted? Isn't there laws that,..." *

"In July of last year, man," Scrounge interjects, "the Good City Council declared a state of public health emergency, which enabled the city to do whatever they wanted to get rid of us, you know? And they tried, you know? In December, the city was giving out tents, like, 60 or 70 of em to have us be setting up on a different city-owned parking lot,..." *

"Yeah,..." interrupts Jerome. "But then a County Judge barred the city from handing out any more tents, and granted a restraining order,..." *

"And," Scrounge says excitedly, "Some business owners sued the city, saying the city didn't follow their own rules or give proper notice." *

"Sounds really complicated." Princess says with a confused look on her face. "Why,..." *

"It's city thinking." Jerome answers. "And that ain't the half of it.

The judge said that those who moved in the new tents before the court ruling can stay, but no one else is allowed in." *

"But why is this happening?" Princess asks. *

"The same reason you're here." Gladstone answers. "Eviction is a leading cause of us being out here on the streets and more than 50 percent of evicted renters in Washington have been kicked out for owing one month or less, in rent." Gladstone pauses. "So, I heard of this guy that was evicted for owing just forty nine dollars; really." *

"And there was another guy," Hoot interjects "that was nearly evicted for owing $2.00." *

"And,..." Faith adds, "Most of them folks being evicted end up having to pay their landlord's court costs and attorney fees." *

"What?" Princess retorts incredulously. "That's outrageous. How can they get away with that?" *

Gladstone continues, "At least in Seattle, landlords have to give a 60-days' notice if they plan to raise the rent by 10 percent or more; but everyone else is screwed." *

"Yeah,..." Scrounge says, looking serious, "I heard from our advocate lawyer that they're supposed to give renters and us here in this place, 90 days to respond to eviction notices." *

"Wait a minute," Princess replies, "You guys got your own lawyer?" *

"Yeah." Jerome answers. "Real nice guy. Sharp. Knows all the

RCWs uh, that is to say, the Revised Codes of Washington for the renter's legal rights, renters also known as tenants, and he's up on all the RCWs for landlords too. He comes in the camps, trying to help us. Really nice guy, but you know the old saying, "you can't fight city hall?" Well, he out there doing it anyway." *

"So, is he a public defender then?" Princess asks. *

"Nah," Jerome answers, "He's doing it all for free. For us. He's a class act." Jerome grins dejectedly and continues, "I was talking to him the other day and he told me about a catch 22; So he went to throw his hat in and to be part of the Thurston County Public Defense, right? And they snubbed him; politely, but they disregarded and refused his services for a past association with another lawyer." *

"Can they do that?" Princess asks. *

"Can and did." Jerome answers. *

"Seems like it's all so unfair for the homeless and their circumstances." Princess replies. *

"Unfair?" Jerome ponders the word and says, "It really all comes down to gentrification." *

"What's that?" Princess asks with a look of confusion. *

"It's the process of renovating and improving a neighborhood or district so that it conforms to upper-class taste." Jerome explains. "In this case, if you can't change the direction of the homeless people, or make the them more acceptable or desirable to everyone driving through the city, you just effect a change to the area, kicking people out or moving them out of sight, all under the guise of improvements, so that things conform to the now, upper-middle-class predilections,..." *

"Predilections." Faith declares, "That is a very good word, Jerome." *

"As I was saying," Jerome says, pointing. "You see that block over there? That's the new mitigation site." Princess looks over as he continues. "Yeah, that's right. It's just one block away. But, it's not here on State Street. Out of sight, problem solved. It's city thinking." *

"Like what they did to the Artesian Park last summer?" Hoot asks. *

"Exactly." Jerome answers, punching the air. "All part of the city's general anti-homeless and their favorite fall back tool of criminalizing tendencies of anything they detect in their way." *

"That's terrible." Princess replies. "You sure they're not just reacting to what's happening?" *

"They know what they're doing." A voice announces from the other side of one of the tents. "Actions or reactions, they've got an extermination plan in play." *

"Hey, Private." Gladstone says to a man that steps up slowly like a person in pain. He is accompanied with a large dog on a leash that, on command, immediately sits next to Private. "How's it going, man?" Gladstone asks. *

"I been better." Private replies. Glancing for a moment at Princess and back to Gladstone. *

Private, tired and weather-worn, looks back at Princess before saying, "Me and Dumpster just out-maneuvered two cops." Private looks apprehensively around. "So, if anybody comes looking for me, I been here, okay?" Private smiles mischievously. *

"What happened?" Scrounge asks. *

"Let's just say," Private speaks with a strained grin, "that I had a difference of opinion with that store over there across from the bus station." *

"That,..." Hoot begins slowly. *

"Hoot,..." Faith interrupts to stop Hoot from perhaps, swearing. Hoot looks back annoyed. *

"I went in there to get me some medicine and they totally freaked out,... again." *

"This happened before?" Princess asks, looking back at Private. *

Faith turns to Princess and says, "The owner is always getting ripped off. So, he especially doesn't like any homeless looking people." Faith looks at Dumpster and smiles. "And no dogs." *

"And especially," Hoot interjects, "anyone that looks overly suspicious; like Private here." *

"He called the cops on you?" Princess asks, "just because he didn't like the way you look?" *

Private looks at Princess without answering. *

"Don't mind him." Gladstone reports. "Private is a man of few words and,..." *

"I'm sorry." Princess says shyly. "I didn't mean,..." *

"Don't." Private replies curtly, raising up one hand. "It's not you, even though I don't know you, but I,... just been having a day ." Private rubs one of his eyes with the heel of his hand, looks up ready to sing, '*Struggling To Get Back*'

19

Struggling To Get Back

Yeah, that was me there sitting on a curb,
chance for breakfast came and went
Meanwhile all of my possessions got stolen out of Bobbie's tent
Going down to the C.C.C. to fend off this chilling cold
And maybe connect with a friend or two,
and share a story told

I'll be sleeping tonight under a bridge
next to the railroad track
Had a bit of bad luck from poor choices
but I'm struggling to get back,
Struggling to get back

Lost my job when they found out
I was recently released
Too bad cause all I really needed was enough money
to catch a bus to go back east

And it's hard to be honest and trustworthy
to deal with how I've come undone
What with so many in survival mode
just looking out for number one

But hey, everybody's got their story
of their hit and run surprise attack
And them that can think straight to form a plan
are struggling to get back.
Yeah, struggling to get back

I remember a time of another place
where I was accepted, and just because
where I had dignity and respect
for who and what I really was
This situation for me is temporary
so I'm singing my blues away
and I'm expecting a change in the weather
to happen most any day; any day

Till then I'm taking care with caution
to get myself back on track
I'm down and out right now my friend,
but I'm struggling to get back.
Yeah, struggling to get back

Private calmly picks up Hoot's 'Guitar with No Strings' and turns his back to everyone while playing out a guitar riff on through to the end of the song.

20

ACT ONE - SCENE SIX

ACT ONE — SCENE SIX:

The Players:
HOOT, GLADSTONE & JEROME

EXT. SIDEWALK: Gladstone, and Hoot are walking to the Community Care Center (CCC) with Jerome who is hurriedly walking well in front of them, talking to himself. *

"….So I'd have to say Faith is a lot closer to that scene than I am." Hoot replies to Gladstone. "I'm on a path that's leading to the,… to there, you know? But I'm just not so,…" *

"Perfect?" Gladstone interjects, looking over with a curious glance. "Faith is maybe the most bestist, caring person I've ever met. She's always doing good things for everybody." *

"No doubt, no doubt." Hoot replies. "Bestest friend, supports me in all my endeavors." *

"Hoot," Gladstone asks, pointing, "Why you bringing your, 'Guitar with No Strings' with you?" *

Hoot smiles and says, "Never know when inspiration comes along when it comes to writing a song." *

Gladstone pulls out his harmonica and plays a quick blues riff and puts it away. *

You're getting good on that, man." Hoot complements. "Seems like just yesterday that you,..." *

"When I left you, I was but the learner." Gladstone reports. "Now I am the master." *

Hoot laughs and says, "That's great, kid. Don't get cocky." *

"How long you been writing songs?" Gladstone asks. *

Hoot scratches his head under his hat for a quick moment and replies, "All my life I guess." *

"You been writing songs that long?" *

"Don't make it sound like I'm Methuselah." Hoot replies with fake annoyance. *

"Uh, sorry." Gladstone responds before asking, "How many songs you got?" *

"Don't know; never counted." Hoot answers. "Hundreds, I guess." Hoot looks over at Gladstone and grins, "That don't mean they're all good, son." *

"Everyone of em I heard is good, Hoot." Gladstone declares. "How do you do it? I mean, does the music come first and you put words to it or do you write the lyrics,...".*

"Poems." Hoot corrects. "The poet in me wants to be recognized separately from the musician in me. He knows that he's part of our creative songwriting team, but as a prolific and insightful writer, he doesn't want to get lost in the shadow of the songwriter's shuffle." *

"Well then" Gladstone postulates, "poems. So what is the process?" *

"Happens both ways." Hoot replies, carefully stepping over what looks to be a dead rat. "Sometimes the words just tumble out of my head and I have to find the right music for em; sometimes I get this idea and I start playing my guitar or keyboard and the mood or the feel of what the words should be, kind a flows out to make a sort of,... marriage, you know? And speaking of marriage, I have written a lot of songs for her over the last 40 years." *

"She must be honored." Gladstone replies. *

"Hope so." Hoot says reflectively. "Anyways, sometimes I might get struck, you know, by something in my life? And as I'm writing the words, the music is already dancing in my head; the inspired pieces; the songs that were meant to be." *

"Inspired?" Gladstone questions. "You mean, like maybe from,... God or something?" *

"Well, yeah,..." Hoot replies. "Sometimes I feel like I am an instrument for and in behalf of my Heavenly Father; like I was put here on earth to do this thing I do; to share with others, to maybe help others with the struggles they're going through." *

"So is that the path you were talking about?" Gladstone asks. *

"Maybe not, '*The*' path,... but yeah, I think it's what I'm supposed to do, along with a lot of other things that I'm supposed to do,... that I'm not doing; like reading scriptures or saying my prayers on a regular basis. There's always room for improvement, even for my wife Faith,..." Hoot pauses, "but I'm sure she will be, maybe the only way I get into heaven." Hoot laughs. "I'll be walking behind her and saying to the gatekeeper, "Hey man, I'm with her." *

Gladstone's face turns sad as he says, "I'm sure gonna miss not being around you two guys." *

"I know. This whole thing has got us at odds with the world." Hoot declares. "But something inside is saying tomorrow? Well, you gotta just knock on that door when the time comes and see what happens." *

"That's another thing I like about you." Gladstone utters. "You're such a thinker." *

"Thinker, huh?" Hoot muses. "That's kind of a high complement, there, Buckaroo, and I thank you for it. And,..." Hoot looks forward to see Jerome is out of hearing distance before saying, "You know, I been meaning to tell you how proud I am of you for that thing you been doing." *

Gladstone stops and enquires, "What thing?" *

Hoot smiles. "You know,... the help and assistance you've been rendering out there to them what are vulnerable and helpless. You know? Coming to their defense in their time of need?" *

"Is this where I end up being unmasked and losing my secret identity?" Gladstone asks smiling. *

"What?" Hoot asks. "What are you talking about?" *

"What are you talking about?" Gladstone parrots. *

"I'm talking about how you go out, late at night, every night," Hoot answers, "walking the streets; making sure others are safe from bad people. It's dangerous, Gladstone, maybe you don't realize,..." *

"It can be,..." Gladstone says looking over at Hoot. "But I know how to move around in the shadows." *

Hoot smiles wryly and says, "You know what? You're kind a like one of your comic-book heroes." *

Gladstone grins and replies, "That's high praise to me." *

"Should be," Hoot replies, "You're living it." *

"You know that girl I told you about?" Gladstone asks quietly. "The one I told you about couple a nights ago? The one I was worried about sleeping in her car?" *

"Oh yeah," Hoot answers, "the one you had to chase Roger away from a couple nights ago? Where you got roughed up a might?" *

"Yeah, that's the one." Gladstone answers, rubbing the side of his ribs. "Don't remind me." *

"That guy's dangerous; and his friends." Hoot says gravely. "You need to steer clear of him." *

"I know." Gladstone smiles. "Anyway, that girl I told you about? *

Yeah," Hoot says, looking up to access his memory, "So?" *

"Turns out that that girl? Gladstone responds questioningly. "It was Princess that was in that car." *

"Really?" Hoot exclaims with a loud, excited whisper. "What'd be the chances?" *

"Yeah, I know." Gladstone answers. "I guess she just kind a got hungry enough to come in today and get something to eat,... and then she sits down across from me at my table, of all the tables in Sally's." *

"Really!" Hoot exclaims. *

Gladstone stops walking, turns to Hoot and declares, "And you won't believe it, but, she had these goons waiting for her when we went back to get her car." *

"What do you mean?" Hoot asks. "She had people waiting for her? Did they try to,…" *

"I don't know what they were up to." Gladstone returns. "Maybe to nab her, or kidnap her. But don't worry; she seen em waiting for her before they even seen her and she ditched em." Gladstone smiles. "I did this clever, reconnaissance thing, and I went to talk to em to see what was going on." Gladstone looks serious as he continues. "One guy said he was her brother, but she says he wasn't." *

Hoot looks somber as he asks, "You think you might be getting in too deep with this one?" *

"This one?" Gladstone parrots. "Since when was there ever someone else?" *

"Point taken." Hoot replies, lifted up a bit. *

"All I can say," Gladstone says as he starts them to walking again, "is that they weren't nice guys." *

Hoot replies. "This could be serious you know." *

"I feel she's a good kid." Gladstone replies sincerely. "She needs help." Hoot smiles knowingly. "And you realize this is probably not just some coincidence, right?" *

"You mean she's trouble and I should steer clear of her?" Gladstone asks. *

"No, not that." Hoot replies. "Well maybe, but what I mean is that the universe works in mysterious ways. I believe it could be a sign that she was, or still is, in some kind of danger, and I think that you two were meant to meet and that perhaps God, or something in the universe is entrusting you to take care of her; at least till she's out of this dilemma." *

"Really?" Gladstone exclaims, "That sounds,..." *

"Crazy?" Hoot interjects. "Be one with the Force and see what it tells you." *

Gladstone laughs, "Don't try to frighten me with your sorcerer's ways. Your sad devotion to that ancient religion has not helped you conjure up a real place to live, or given you clairvoyance enough to realize any legal strategies to stop the city from evicting us,..." *

Hoot laughs as he contorts his left hand and says, "I find your lack of faith disturbing." *

Gladstone holds his throat like he's being choked. They both laugh together. *

"What'd I miss?" Jerome asks as Hoot and Gladstone continue walking and laughing. *

21

ACT ONE - SCENE SEVEN

ACT ONE — SCENE SEVEN

Players:
FAITH, PRINCESS, SCROUNGE,
ANGEL & BOBBY

EXT. THE MITIGATION SITE, TENT SEMICIRCLE: Faith, Scrounge, Angel and Princess are hanging back at the encampment in the Circle, tidying up and making themselves more presentable. Scrounge is searching between tents, foraging in the debris for anything of value as Angel sits half in and half out of her tent, reading a comic book, facing Princess who is sitting on a 5-gallion bucket as Faith stands behind Princess, braiding her hair. "City's gonna win this time." Faith says to Princess. They're anxious to break up our thing." *

"Thing?" Questions Princess. *

"Yeah;" Scrounge answers. "Our rag-tag group; our commune, our little district here, this population of tent people; our world-weary society. They know when they break us up, it's almost impossible to regather ourselves to somewhere else, especially when they regulate through their lottery system who's going into the tents at the new mitigation site," Scrounge looks around, "And who does not. They want to instill a continued sense of uncertainty and fear to the lot of us, and they want to fracture our sense of community. In short, they want us gone." *

"So, they're afraid of you guys?" Princess asks. *

"Not you guys;" Faith corrects. "Us guys. And not afraid so much, but terribly concerned about control, of which they do not have. But, they hold all the cards here and they know it." Faith gazes over the sea of tents and continues. "And yeah, they're thinking,.. more like hoping, we'll all go somewhere else, leave their city alone and this all goes away." Faith makes a face like she's straining as she gathers a huge bunch of Princess's hair and continues. "But there's no rest for the weary. Seattle is transporting their homeless down here to Olympia and that can't help our plight. Meanwhile, in LA there's over fifty-four thousand homeless people and it's more every month as landlords continue to raise their rents, unregulated." *

"This all makes me mad." Angel interjects. "It's not fair." *

"Fair is in the eyes of the beholder." Scrounge say's from behind a group of tents. *

"What you doing round my tent?" A voice calls out from inside a tent. *

"Woah," Scrounge says loudly startled. "I didn't know you were in, Bobby." *

"Good thing I was." Bobby replies as she exits her tent and stands up. "otherwise maybe more a my stuff might a gone missing." *

"We already been around that block." Scrounge replies. "And I don't like to be called a thief." *

"Shoe fits?" Bobby says coyly as she steps up to where Princess and Faith are sitting. *

"This is Princess." Angel replies. "Princess? This is Bobby; She's a boxer." *

"Thank you, Angel, for not saying, female boxer." Bobby says appreciatively. *

"And I get it." Faith continues, ignoring Bobby and Scrounge. Faith puts some finishing touches on Princess's French braid and says, "Homeowners and landlord's costs keep going up too. Plumbing, carpentry, electrical, you name it. And they're just trying to make a living too." *

"But," Scrounge interjects, "many of them; not all of em, but there are some out there that get the, "dollar signs in the eyes" affliction as their bank accounts grow and they just want more." *

Faith stands and says, "You coming with us, Bobby? We're heading over to the CCC." *

"Yeah," Bobby replies, glancing at Scrounge with suspicion. "I gotta wash what's left of my clothes." *

22

ACT ONE - SCENE EIGHT

ACT ONE — SCENE EIGHT:

Players:
**FAITH, PRINCESS, HOOT, GLADSTONE,
BOBBY, PRIVATE, JEROME & SCROUNGE**

INT. THE COMMUNITY CARE CENTER (CCC): "So," Faith says to Princess as they step into a large open-spaced building, "This is the Community Care Center (we call it, "the CCC"). It's owned by the local hospital. As you probably saw as we walked in, the CCC has that outdoor area out there that we just walked through; people hang out there until they open the doors at ten." Faith points to an L shaped front desk where there is a long line of people waiting. "The whole place is run by a community of churches." Faith reports. "They have a bunch of paid and volunteer workers helping to run the place. The staff treats everyone with respect and dignity." *

As Princess walks in she sees a bunch of round tables scattered around the small auditorium-like room where between five to eight people sit at or stand next to. There are people next to the walls and in corners lying on the floors sleeping; some with and some without sleeping bags.. *

A man in the coffee line is pushing a baby carriage filled with plastic bags full of stuff. There's a guest making the coffee as the workers are overwhelmed.

A man with a cat perched on his shoulder, walks through the crowd pulling a large overstuffed traveling suitcase with squeaky wheels. He steps right in front of Princess who swerves to avoid bumping into him, only to almost trip on a woman that is lying on the floor doing sit-ups in the main walkway.

An older man with little to no coordination is playing soccer scrimmage with a hacky-sack, weaving in between chairs and tables.

There's a woman walking around the tables and asking if she can have the thing she's found on the table. She finds herself confused as she is suddenly barraged and overwhelmed by the din of everyone seemingly talking at once with voices in mid sentences, in need of, but without anyone to listen to them..*

One voice says, "...I love being treated like a five-year-old in my own place,..." and, "...I'm confused. I been time shifting and I don't know what,..." and, "...I can't believe you did that, what's wrong with you,..." and, "...I know how to go in white and black, my tricks,..." and, "...I told you, I'm only the wingman,..." and, "...but paying to be a preacher?,..." and, "You're gonna be my mentor,..." and, "...That ain't right. We used to,..." and, "...Jesus knew what he was doing, Matthew, Mark, Luke and John? Come on. They're the constant,..." and, "...threw me off the bus,..." and, "...last place I seen her,..." and, "...he got beat up bad,..." and, "...you tell them I ain't giving it back,...Michael knows, you know that,..." and, "I'm wearing my best face for the day," and, "It's always been about the,... no, it has to be in a certain order to be,..." *

Unexpectedly, a tall thin woman with crooked teeth and tired but piercing eyes steps up to Princess, looks her in the face and says, "I know about the infrared satellites and the anti-infrared satellites; I know they want to put a chip inside me; the improved chip with the Wi-Fi broadcaster so they'll know where I am at all times." Her smile disappears and she says, "Above the law? Police will take action, I guarantee it." *

Princess, confused, says, "I'm sorry, did I,..." *

"It's a counsel job on the line,..." The woman says with determination. "You'll get to get in on all the fun. By the way," The woman looks away and smiles, saying, "if that happens, I don't need a license,..." and trailing off, Princess hears her saying, ",...twenty four bucks is twenty four bucks, so tell me,..." *

Faith takes Princess by the hand and pulls her out of the center of the aisleway, leans over to her ear and says, "It can be intense in here sometimes, you okay?" *

"Yeah," Princess answers. "It was kind of weird, like I was hearing everyone thinking all at once." *

"Good analogy." Faith replies. "A lot of these folks, because they're not taking their meds or because they are, or because some of them have their serious mental issues; but they are literally thinking out loud." *

"That woman over there,..." Princess points, "She seemed to know me or,..." *

"Jenifer." Gladstone replies from behind Princess. "She's got issues." *

"And," Bobby interjects, looking around the room, "the homeless have high rates of mental illness, substance abuse, and previous incarcerations; it's what puts a lot of these folks on the street and into homelessness." *

"Good thing is," Faith says smiling, "from what I know about you, which is not much, you're not a stranger to the kind of behavior that goes on in here. And some of these people gravitate to you because their blight spirits see the light in your heart; they can see your goodness. We must be careful." *

"They got washers and dryers over there and,..." Gladstone says pointing to a caged area. "And,... you gotta get on a list to get to take a shower. That's why Hoot was so anxious to get here early." *

"Over here, friends." Hoot yells, waving his hands, from a table where he is seated. *

"Wow, there sure are a lot of people here." Princess says as she gets to the table and sits next to Gladstone. Princess asks, "Are all these people here homeless?" *

"Yeah, mostly." Replies Gladstone. "Last year, 552,830 people were counted homeless in the United States, leaving the most vulnerable, dependent on the government – or the mercy of the streets." *

"Of course," Bobby says, sitting down at the table. "Almost half of all unsheltered homeless people are found in California, mostly San Francisco, LA, Santa Rosa, and San Jose; with Seattle being next." Bobby grins as she continues, "But East Coast cities have the highest rate of homelessness; more than 20 percent of all homeless people live in New York City." *

"That doesn't make sense." Princess says. "It sounds like faulty math." *

"There's a difference between unsheltered and semi sheltered homeless." Bobby answers.".*

"And," Gladstone interjects, "there are predators out there too." *

"Predators?" Princess asks. *

"Yeah." Hoot answers. "Scumbags that come here looking to take advantage of the new faces. A lot of times they're not even homeless, but they look the part and speak the lingo." *

"Prime targets for predators." Gladstone continues. "After you been here for a while you get to know who they are and stay away from em, but until you do, you're their victim." *

"They bring in the drugs at a very cheap price," Hoot replies, "all with a promise of relief that so many feel they need; only to hook you and scheme you out of whatever money you got or for sex and,..." *

"Come on," Princess interrupts. "Really? These folks are already down and out. How could,..." *

"Real simple." Hoot says, helping Faith to set up her laptop. "Scumbags." *

"Hoot." Faith says sternly. "I wish you'd stop using that word." *

Hoot smiles and asks, "Okay my wordologist; would you rather I said, contemptible? Or maybe loathsome? Or how about shameful? Or appalling,... or maybe vile, or what about just plain awful?" *

"Don't play with me." Faith counters. "You know what I mean. I think we all get the picture here." *

"Maybe." Hoot replies, rolling his eyes dismissively. *

"So, Bobby; did you get a spot to wash your stuff?" Faith asks. *

"No; I'm on a second list for the afternoon." Bobby answers. "Might end up being a lottery thing." *

Across the room, a tall man with dreadnaught hair and long disheveled beard is speaking threateningly to Jerome. "You don't know what you're talking about." The man says threateningly. "And I think,..." *

Private, with his dog Dumpster on leash, seems to come out from nowhere and quickly steps in between Jerome and the other man before saying, "Let it go, Roger. Jerome didn't do anything to you." *

"I don't like him." Roger says. "He keeps spouting off ridiculous stuff that makes no sense,..." Roger turns and faces Private. "And I don't like you either. Why don't you mind your own business?" *

As Private moves closer to Roger's face, almost to the point of touching noses, Dumpster growls softly. Private says, "Jerome is a big part of my family; ergo, he is my business." *

Roger looks down at the dog and then back up at Private and says, "Listen, old man, you best to go back to your rocking chair before I have to put a hurt on you." *

Dumpster growls louder and more threateningly. Private looks down at Dumpster smiling and says, "Hey buddy, I got this." The dog stops growling but remains on guard. Private's smile disappears as he looks back into Roger's eyes before he says, "And just to let you know, *this* old man can take you outside and clean your clock in a heartbeat; if you're looking for an invitation, let's go; right now." *

Seeing the determination in Private's countenance, a look of fear washes over Roger's face, but after looking around the room, Roger sees all the people looking at him and he quickly regains his composure. "Another time, old man." Roger quips. "I got business to attend to." *

Roger steps slowly back and then walks away. On his way to a table over by the washers, he passes by Hoot's table and glances over at Princess and he licks his lips as he smiles. But the smile is short lived when he sees Princess is sitting with Gladstone, who looks up at Roger with steel resolve, as if to say, "Not this time; not this one." Roger's smile is replaced with a look of contempt. *

"That was Roger's "fresh meat" look that you just got." Gladstone says to Princess. "Until he saw you were with me,... or uh, us." Gladstone looks around and smiles. "You're in a safe zone for now." *

"Yuck." Princess says as she moves her chair even closer to Gladstone, so as to accommodate fitting in Jerome and Private at the table. Dumpster lays down on the floor next to Private. "He was so,... so, smarmy." Says Princess. *

"Smarmy." Faith parrots without looking up from her computer, "That's a very good word." *

"Good word or not," Gladstone interjects, "you be careful. In his mind, he ain't done with you yet. Roger is like a lion that preys on stragglers. You need to stay away from him." *

"Like I'd want to have anything to do with him." Princess says with furled brows. *

Dumpster gets up from his laying-down stance and moves next to Bobby, rubbing her legs in hopes of getting her attention. *

"I swear," Private comments, smiling wryly, "I do believe that that dog went to the wrong tent when he first arrived here." *

"You may be right." Bobby agrees with a knowing smile. "I don't think I was home at the time. So, sad to say, that would make you his second choice." *

Scrounge steps up to the table and throws down a collection of magazines. "Slim pickings." She says as she pulls up a seat to be next to Angel. "Someone else must a gotten to Sidewalk first." *

"You *are* an hour late, mother." Angel says. "You know the old saying, "early bird" thingy." *

"So, these were all out on the sidewalk?" Princess asks. *

"No dear." Faith answers with a short glance up. "Sidewalk is an advocacy for the homeless to get into housing so they won't be homeless or as Jerome might say, houseless anymore." *

"Houseless is a better generic term." Jerome interjects. "We don't have a house or apartment to live in but my tent, for all practical purposes, is my home for now." *

"Well played." Private says, shooting an approval look to Jerome. *

"Really?" Hoot says, holding up a magazine. "Melissa McCarthy?" *

"What?" Private asks. *

"Okay, I get it." Hoot announces. "I can see, Bruce Springsteen, or Sally Fields, or Martin Short, or Diane Keaton, or Patrick Stewart, or even Tom Hanks even though he was born in 56, but Melissa McCarthy? Or Brad Pitt, or Luke Parry? Or Johnny Depp for goodness sake? I mean it used to mean something for you to be honored with being on the cover of the AARP." *

"Here we go again." Faith says wearily without looking up. *

Hoot stands up with the attention of the room on him, he raises 'the guitar without strings' and begins playing the song; '*On The Cover Of The AARP*'

23

On The Cover Of
The AARP

I've been working real hard to get me this far
But I'm still mostly unknown
And in a nobody stance there ain't really much chance
Of me on the cover of the Rolling Stone
Hey, hey, hey, but don't touch that dial,
I been out here for a while
Doing the Lord Baldwin shuffle for free
Armed with classic rock and roll; I got me a new goal
To be on the cover of the AARP,... the AARP

With an old hippie smile I been out here for a while
Infusing songs with blood, sweat and tears
Now, if it's my time to be I gotta let em all see
What I been doing all these years.
Meanwhile, I can see my story inside, buried on page thirty-five

above an ad for Medicare that I'm gonna need
Somebody's bound to say, 'who's that guy anyway
On the cover of the AARP' The AARP

I'd like to see my picture on the cover,
wanna prove to all my brothers
That I wasn't really just wasting my life.
I'd like to see my picture up there,
like to think that somebody would care
that I'm still out there doing my thing
and that I'm still alive.

With them over sixty-five there's no shuck and jive
They're just trying to adjust after the retire
They don't know my sign, the who or what or why
I'm still singing bout a World On Fire.
When I can be Googled with love, on Wikipedia
The world will know a little more about me,...
So I'm singing for you, hoping you'll approve
Of me being on the cover of the AARP,...
On the cover of the AARP

Uh, the AA, ADC, no, AP uh, AARP
It's a memory thing, you know, it comes and it goes,...

24

ACT ONE - SCENE NINE

ACT ONE — SCENE NINE:

The Players:
**FAITH, PRINCESS, HOOT, GLADSTONE,
BOBBY, PRIVATE, JEROME & SCROUNGE**

INT. THE COMMUNITY CARE CENTER (CCC): "You guys keep carrying on," Bobby interjects, "but tomorrow morning we're all gonna get kicked out of the Circle. And none of us except Faith and Hoot got anywhere to go." *

"I'm happy for Hoot and Faith though,…" Scrounge says as she looks over at them. "I mean, getting into the new mitigation site." A sad smile crosses her face as she continues. "But I am sure gonna miss both of em." *

"I think we're all gonna miss each other." Hoot declares, hoping to waylay his wife's oncoming sadness. "We need to somehow keep in touch so we can stay close forever." Hoot looks at Princess and says, "That includes you too, kid. You're now an honorary mouseketeer." Hoot leans towards Faith and says, "Tell you what. We'll create a database or a spreadsheet or something that has information about everybody in the Circle and then we'll email everybody a copy. Does that sound good?" *

"Hoot," Faith says excitedly as she looks unbelievingly at Hoot with furrowed brows, "That's a great idea." *

"I know, I know." Hoot replies with pretended pride, "Sometimes I can be brilliant." *

Faith scrambles with her mouse and laptop, creating the spreadsheet and then turns to Private and says, "I'm gonna start with you, Private. I already got your email address. Do you have any idea where you might be going tomorrow?" *

"The VA was supposed to get back to me by now," Private answers, "but as you know, I'm not on anybody's, 'A' list right now." *

"What does that mean?" Princess asks with concern. *

"Lot of veterans are homeless;" Private answers. "A lot with conditions worse than mine and a lot of them are like me, out on the streets. I gotta feel sorrier for them than I do for myself. I can still get around. I can't work due to my increased disabilities but my compensation and pension are enough for me to sustain myself now. I ended up on the streets, but those guys in the VA know I've digressed from the last time I was "probed" so, it's a waiting game.

I'm just hoping they'll get to me when it's my time" Private loughs and says, "Hopefully not wait till my time is up."*

Princess watches Faith typing in information and sees Private's email address. She asks, "What does Yooper49 mean?" *

Private pets his dog, smiles wryly and says, "I'm from Iron Mountain, Michigan. And, Michigan is actually two different pieces of land, separated by lake Michigan and Lake Huron." Private pulls out his phone and brings up a map of Michigan. "And see here?" He says pointing to the map, "This part is called the mitt or glove, for obvious reasons, and this part up here where Iron Mountain is called the upper peninsula. Upper peninsula folks are called, Yoopers." Private purses his lips. *

"I didn't mean to make you sad." Princess says receptively. *

Private looks down and smiles. "It wasn't you. I was just thinking about a place not far from my home that brought back memories of another time and place,…" Private now stands up and looking far and away, sings; **'Bobcat Ridge'**

25

Bobcat Ridge (Revisited)

I couldn't wait to get away from that one-horse town
Move out on my own and start to really get around
And it's funny how life's better down the road, far away
Till from miles gone by, you look back from where you came
And many years and miles have found me at this place
A far cry from home; too far, too long, too late
And I think of that life and all the things we did
When we were young and innocent,
up on Bobcat Ridge

I left Suzanne waiting while I had to find myself
I imagine after all these years, she's with somebody else
And I still regret my leaving her, and I sometimes wonder why
But I cannot change the past and all the time that passed by
And many years and miles have found me at this place
A far cry from happy in this treadmill race
But I think back at times, and all the things we did

When we were young and innocent,
up on Bobcat Ridge

Some have measured my success by my station in life
how much money's in the bank and the car that I drive
but they cannot see the man that sacrificed and lost it all
who's one wish is to go back to a place now long gone
Too many years and miles have found me at this place
I'm a far cry from happy. Too far, too long, too late
But there's times I think back, when I was a kid
and I'm there with all my friends,
up on Bobcat Ridge
Bobcat Ridge

Private scans everyone's faces for acceptance and his eyes stops when he reaches Bobby,... Private is hoping most of all that Bobby might understand him and his plight a bit better,... Bobby looks back into Private's eyes knowingly, with a fire of empathy, (and maybe love),... Private smiles softly as he moves out of the limelight and motions for Dumpster to come with him,... Dumpster, who has been by Bobby's side during the song, looks back at Private with a look that says, "I think I'd like to hang out for a while with Bobby here,..." Bobby raises her eyebrows and smiles,... Private fake grimaces before saying, "I know what you mean" and Private walks back to his tent.

26

ACT ONE - SCENE TEN

The Players:
FAITH, PRINCESS, HOOT, GLADSTONE,
BOBBY, PRIVATE, JEROME & SCROUNGE

INT. THE COMMUNITY CARE CENTER (CCC): Private says nothing as he sits back down next to Bobby, looks down on the dog, before he scratches behind Dumpster's ears. *

"That sounded magical, Private, thank you." Bobby says softly. "I was deeply moved." *

Hearing Bobby's voice, Dumpster sits up and leaning, rubs his head on her leg. "That's a good boy." Bobby says smiling at Private as she too scratches behind Dumpster's ears. *

"There you go again." Private says with pretended anger. "Stealing my dog." *

"He really does like you, Bobby." Princess replies. *

"As for you Princess," Faith inquires, "What information can I glean from you?" *

"I got an email address." Princess reports, "but I got nothing else for you. I mean, even if my brother's car was still there with all my stuff in it, I don't dare go back for fear they; whoever they are, would-be lying-in wait. I think what's happened is; after I never showed up to be reevaluated, my mother probably signed the papers to have me picked up to be committed to Western. Either that or that was an ambush set up to accomplish some other unknown end by some other unknown force. Neither of which am I ready or willing to succumb to." *

"Succumb?" Faith parrots. "That's a pretty good word." *

"Let me paint you a different scenario, if I may." Jerome says excitedly. "You had a troubled mind. And recently you spent time in a State institution until they deemed you well, right?" *

"Yeah,..." Princess answers. "But what,..." *

"What does that have to do with the price of tea in China?" Jerome interjects, "Just this. Your name, your identity, your essence is all written down in some files at some facility. Now, most people believe that Health Insurance Portability and Accountability Act (HIPAA) laws keep our medical records private, shared only amongst our doctors, ourselves, and maybe a loved one or caregiver.

But those who believe that will be surprised to learn that others have access to their records and don't need anyone's consent to do so. And, if you went to see other physicians, they would need access to those files and, thanks to Adobe and the internet, all your files; "your very essence," was digitized in a series of PDF and JPG files; access to those files could have been granted to anyone with a minimal degree of clearance. Sound feasible?" *

"Well yes," Princess answers nervously. "I guess it could have been like that,..." *

"I think you're frightening her." Gladstone interrupts. *

"Good, Good." Jerome retorts. "If I was in her shoes I'd at least be concerned if not intimidated too." Jerome turns to Gladstone and continues. "Don't you see? The license plate number? The vertical "XMT" and the letter "C" on the end? Only Government vehicles have sets of "exempt" license plates, denoted by a small vertical "XMT" on the left side of the plate. Government vehicles belonging to counties, end with a "C" and ones belonging to municipalities, end in "D." The state's confidential license plate program is designed to protect undercover law enforcement, to protect the safety of government workers or elected officials and the program is limited to law enforcement purposes." *\

Jerome looks in both directions before continuing, "But let's review some other simple facts: Aside from the fact that they're driving a government issued windowless cargo van with a cage, (used to transport prisoners or dangerous folks), those men did not identify themselves when you encountered them. They lied to you about who they were, (of course, not unusual for anyone working for the government), then they tried to trick you into giving them information about who you were, of which, I'm really happy, Gladstone that you did not relent. They don't like your kind of free thinking." *

"Your point,..." Gladstone begins, impatiently. *

"My point is," Jerome answers, "Princess here is being sought by some rogue agent or some private government agency for some un-known reason. That in itself should be concerning, but there's some other facts to be weighed. First, Princess has left the grid." Jerome turns to Princess and asks, "Princess, how often were you supposed to check back in for your reevaluations, and when was it that you had your last appointment? Approximately." *
"Every three months." Princess answers, seeming more curious than scared. "And about six months ago." *

"So," Jerome says and pauses, turning away, nodding his head like he's actively thinking,... then Jerome suddenly turns back around and says, "So Princess you've been off the grid for more than 90 days. That, Princess is the very thing that scares the holy batman and robin out of the collective." *

"The collective?" Hoot parrots comically with a smile. "Better shed some light on that one." *

Jerome gives Hoot a serious glance before returning his attention to the crowd. He turns his head to the left and says, "So, you want to be a democrat? Go ahead. Register as such and the government says, we'll document it." He turns his head to the right and says, "You wanna be a republican? Go ahead. Register as such and we'll docu-ment it." He looks right at Faith but more like he's looking through her and says, "You wanna be a member of a church? You want religion, do you? Go ahead. Register as such and we'll document it."

Jerome's voice gets stronger as he looks at Scrounge before saying, "You want your kids to go to school? Go ahead. Register as such and we'll document it." He looks down for a moment and says, "You wanna drive a car?" Jerome looks up and into each person's face for a moment before turning away again and saying, "Go ahead. Register as such and we'll document it."

Jerome turns to Princess and says, "Princess, I think their fault was that they underestimated you." Jerome seems to look into Princess's soul before saying, "It's obvious that you are one of the Specials." *

Gladstone's face suddenly pops up with surprise. *

Princess looks bewildered. *

Seeing the reaction on Princess's face, Jerome holds up his hands in surrender before saying, "And I mean that in a very respectful way. A "Special" has a power; and I don't know what that power is, only that a "Special's" power can upset the balance and that worries some folks." *

"I've read about the, 'Specials.'" Gladstone replies. *

"Yeah," Scrounge interjects, "In some comic book." *

"Don't you be fooled," Jerome says, turning to Scrounge. "There's a lot of covert information out there in comics; you just need to know where to look and what to read." *

"Sounds like,..." Private says softly, looking down at Dumpster, "I don't know,... science fiction?" *

"Let me continue if I may." Jerome says. "My first guess is that they are just starting to get nervous over not finding you to put you back into your matrix life-tube where you will be drugged to go back to your life-inside-a-life sleep so you will think true thoughts, no more. Not to mention that they know you now, and of your potential, and, you can bet your sweet Tiera that if they ever catch back up with you again, they will never give you another chance to get away." *

"This is,..." Hoot replies, speaking hesitantly and slow, "kind a wild, Jerome, even for you." *

Jerome gives Hoot another serious glance, takes a deep breath, turns to Princess and says, "When you left the grid, couple of good things happened to you that you may or may not be aware of." *

Princess looks into Gladstone's face and smiles. *

"No, no." Jerome says incredulously. "Not that." Jerome looks for a quick moment at Hoot who sends him a, "How do you know it's not love?" glance back. Jerome turns dubiously back to Princess and says, "Well, maybe that too, but what I'm talking about is; speculating of course, but I think someone on the inside has purposely mixed up or corrupted your files. That means there's someone on the inside, one of the good guys, is looking out for you. How else would you have been cleared to be released after you were committed? That doesn't happen so much." *

"Really?" Princess asks with a knowing glance. *

"And, one other thing," Jerome continues, ignoring Princess, "Being here, with all of the homeless; you're in the land of the lost. You are no longer on the government's radar. Well we are all on somebody's radar unfortunately, but most of these people, even Private with his military background; we're all pretty much unaccounted for." *

"Are you trying to scare me?" Princess askes with a glare. *

"Do you think you have reason to be scared?" Jerome asks. *

"Maybe." Princess replies with a note of unsureness. *

"Well there, you're kind of okay,..." Jerome replies with a queer smile. "They; the city, the state, the federal government, they are all burdened with and embarrassed by the fact that there are things that they could do, should do to end our plight,... but they don't. And I'd be surprised if they sent their Storm Troopers into these camps to try to find someone. If this homeless thing won't go away than they'll just cut us off from help and let us all run around like rats in the garbage and eventually, one by one, either kill each other off or just dwindle away." *

Princess looks up at Jerome and then around the table, into each of the faces of her new family before asking, "Why? Why are they doing this?" *

"They're scared, mostly." Hoot replies. "They see us as shabby, loathsome freeloaders and contemptable parasites that have churlish manners, with venal tendencies, our attire, dirty or at least unpleasant, reeking of garbage, and as you saw earlier, they feel us to be unappreciative and thankless for all that they think they're doing for us." *

"You been working on that for a while?" Faith asks curiously with a wry smile. *

"Yeah," Hoot admits, "I have." *

"Well kudos and esteem to you, honey." Faith replies. "And, just cherry picking from all those nouns, verbs and adjectives; my favorites are; loathsome, contemptable, parasites, oh, and the two best favorites; venal and churlish?" She smiles and repeats questioningly, "Churlish? Venal? Hard to believe you know what those words mean but," She raises her hand and says pointedly, "Exceptional Hoot, exceptional." *

"Thank you, thank you very much." Hoot replies trying to sound like Elvis. *

Princess looks over at Jerome and says, "I think I see why they hate us; if I can include myself in this conversation being recently reduced to my present state of affairs, and I get that this place is a health hazard as it is, but what do they gain by closing down one place only to recreate it in another?" *

"Control." Jerome answers. "Control,... and they'll do anything to anyone at anytime to get their way,... and they're everywhere in the shadows,...." *

Jerome stands and turns to face the people at the table and sings; **'They're Taking Over'**

27

They're Taking Over

They were always there for us to endorse or disapprove
Yeah, they were waiting for the right moment
that they could make their move
Biding time in the shadows till conditions were feeling right
Then stepping forward with resolve,
pushing the opposition aside
They're taking over; they're taking over now
Yeah, they're taking over; they're taking over now

We played down the threats, we ignored any warning signs
As they systematically played out their covert plans and designs
Moving from the sidelines, gathering support along the way
Till they got everyone's attention as they took the center stage
They're taking over; they're taking over now
They're taking over; they're taking over now

At first we think what harm is giving them a little bit of choice

After all, they have certain rights to exercise their voice
But they go from simple questioning
to demanding what it is they need
And they push all aside to get to where they planned to be
Now, they're taking over; they're taking over now
Oh, they're taking over; they're taking over now

A simple word, a kind idea that seemed to resonate a true
Mingled with a vague philosophy
to exclude the likes of me and you
And it goes from simple games
to rising up to uphold their stand
And then pushing all aside
to get to where they feel that they'd planned
Oh no,...

What is it that upsets you? Do you feel threatened by their air
As the winds of change are blowing
in their direction everywhere
Maybe you feel weak as they step forward, fresh and strong
Or maybe you feel threatened;
you feel your ways may soon be gone
Maybe it's their empowerment
that grows stronger with every day
Or you fear, the loss, the changes of things
that will never be the same
Whatever it is, you better just get over it friend,
cause they ain't going away
No, they're taking over; they're taking over now
Oh, they're taking over; over now
Yeah, yeah, they're taking over; over now
They're taking over; they're taking over now.

28

ACT ONE - SCENE ELEVEN

The Players:
PRIVATE, SCROUNGE, ANGEL, PRINCESS,
GLADSTONE, FAITH, HOOT, BOBBY & JEROME

INT. THE COMMUNITY CARE CENTER (CCC) (Closing): Private stands and lightly taps on the leash and the dog, lying on the floor next to Bobby, appearing to be sleeping, shoots straight up, moves to Private's side and sits at attention. Private looks triumphantly over at Bobby who fake grimaces back. Private looks down on the dog and smiles as the two of them start walking away from the table. He turns to Bobby and says, "Coming?" *

Bobby looks back disappointedly and says, "Nah, I gotta get in a run before dinner every day." *

"Another time, then?" Private asks. *

"For sure." Bobby replies. "Someone's gotta make sure you're treating that dog right." *

"Later." Private says as he walks away. *

"It's almost five," Scrounge says not so softly. "We gotta get going. Mission's at five thirty and the last time we didn't go early they ran outta some of the food that I was looking forward to eating. *

She looks over at Angel and says, "Come on, we need to go." Scrounge shakes like she's shivering even though in the day room of the CCC it's 75 degrees. *

"I think I'm just gonna go back to the tent." Angel replies. *

"No, no, no," Scrounge says quickly. "Come on, come on, come on,..." *

"Mom, you know I just can't. I got the blues bad. You know,..." Angel says pleadingly, "What we talked about?" Angel asks frowning with impatience. *

"Oh,...," Scrounge answers knowingly, blinking her eyes like she has suddenly woken up. "I got you,... I got you,..." Scrounge stops shaking and stands still. "Okay honey." She says, "I'll bring you back some food." *

"Thanks Mom,,.." Angel says happily but with an air of melancholy. "Could you look for an apple?" *

Scrounge gives a knowing nod and says, "I will. Hey, come on, Angel, I'll walk you back to the Circle." *

"Thanks mom." Angel says happily looking like she was hoping her mother would ask. *

Announcements are given by the Inner Faith crew that the CCC will be closing in ten minutes. Almost immediately, there is a slow sea of people working their way out the door. Jerome nods and as he walks out the door, he is joined with and is talking animatedly with what appears to be, another conspiracy theorist. Hoot picks up his guitar and waits as Faith stands and packs up her gear. They motion to Princess that it's time to go, so she stands and positions herself next to Gladstone who, feeling that he needs to continue with the mantle of the 'Guardian,' walks slowly but vigilantly behind the entourage to their destination. *

29

ACT ONE - SCENE TWELVE

Players:
SCROUNGE, ANGEL, PRINCESS,
GLADSTONE, FAITH, HOOT & BOBBY

EXT. THE TENT CIRCLE: After arriving at the Circle, Scrounge hugs Angel before bolting to the Mission. Angel goes to her tent but stands outside looking up at the stars. Hoot and Faith go inside their tent. *

Princess is standing by Gladstone, next to his tent. *

Bobby arrives, running into camp. "I just ran a half a mile." She says out of breath to anyone listening as she goes into her tent. She emerges quickly after changing her clothes, and as she begins run-walking, she says over her shoulder, "See you over at the Mission." *

"I don't know,.." Princess says nervously to Gladstone. "I'm kind of afraid to go in that place." *

Gladstone looks over knowingly and say, "I got some Cheerios and boxes of milk in my tent; you wait here and I'll go get em if you'd like." *

"I think I would like that," Princess replies softly, "Thank you,..." *

As Gladstone goes into his tent, Princess moves over to Angel's tent and knocks on the canvas like she's knocking on a wooden door. "Hello?" Princess softly calls in. "Hey, you wanna talk?" *

There's a sound of a long zipper and Angel steps out. "Hi." Angel says shyly. *

"I was kind of wondering," Princess says, "if there's anything I might do to be of help to you." *

"Well," Angel says just above a whisper, "I don't know. I don't wanna,..." *

"I just want you to know," Princess relies, "I think I know this is about being a girl." *

"This is all about being sixteen," Angel confesses. "You know?" Angel looks to a space away from looking Princess in the face. "I knew it was coming; I'm not stupid." She steps a bit to the right to put less of an enmity between them and taking a step, says,

"Thing is," she says looking Princess in her face, "I been here in this place long enough to see what it does. And my mom understands, she really does." Angel looks up and says, "The stars are so bright tonight." *

"So, love?" Princess asks with a note of relaxed confidence that she knows the answer. *

Angel nods and does a kind of move swaying back and forth, her hands held in close like she's dancing to a tune, maybe to add doubt that her earlier effort might have been part of a routine and not a nod. *

"You know?" Princess says, standing casually. "I spent a lot of time in places,... Hospitals where the staff was verbally abusive to me and others there. Our conditions were talked about loudly in the hallways and we could hear everything. Some staff were kind, and I also got to talk to a lot of doctors. In fact, after a while I liked it a lot. Some of them thought of me as a nut case; kind a like some of those unfortunates at the CCC. I could tell,... they would treat me like I was five and like, nothing was going on in my life and like, nothing was ever gonna matter anyway." Princess smiles. "But I did like talking to the doctors, you know what I mean?" *

Angel nods with a small concerning smile.*

"And the doctors that believed me,..." Princess continues, "that believed there was a person inside this body that is me? Those were the ones I learned the most from." Princess laughs. "You know,... there were some doctors that even talked to me about some of their other cases, and, by the way," She says tilting her head and opening her eyes, "they're not supposed to do that, you know? But the thing is," Princess looks off and away, "I think I helped some of those doctors more than they ever did for me. Uh,... a doctor would ask me what I'd do in one of his patient's situations and more times than I can know, the doctors listened to me and,... all these other people in the place were getting better. They were so much better that they were getting to leave." *

"But what about you?" Angel called, lifting her head up to air her neck. *

"Yeah,... what about me? Well, after a while, I kind a knew I could leave at any time; but I also felt that if I left, them other folks in there might be there forever." Princess looks straight ahead like she's watching an action movie and says, "Be there forever. So, I stayed till I wasn't needed there anymore and then convinced the good doctors to talk to the bad doctors so the good doctors would let me out." *

"Wow,..." Angel says surprised, "that's incredible." *

"Yeah, yeah," Princess says and smiles as Gladstone draws near. "But that's not the point." She turns her head to face Angel and says, "Like I say, I learned a lot of brain stuff talking to the doctors,..." She pauses then says, "I know how to have you take out some of the pain from the blues; won't take em all out, not completely,..." Princess looks down. "No," she says, "some of your blue stays with you in your heart and soul forever. But anyways, if you're interested, the doctor's in." *

"Well, what do I gotta do?" Angel asks. *

"Okay,..." Princess replies. "I don't need a name but I want you to imagine a paper heart in front of you; we'll call it the 'Paper Heart Spirit' and written across that heart is the name of the person that is affecting your vibes, love vibes, negative vibes, hurting vibes. Can you do that for me, Angel?" *

"Yes." Angel replies. *

"Okay," Princess says with more energy in her voice. "Now imagine that when you and the 'Paper Heart Spirit' are walking together and it makes you feel good to be with the 'Paper Heart Spirit,' you're both happy to be together most of the time. Meanwhile, you have a hard time using the word "love" because it's a new thing and it's supposed to mean so much, so you can't say it; but you do feel it and it feels so different than you thought it would. Sometimes you're not comfortable with the 'Paper Heart Spirit' because,..." The tone of Princess's voice changes to be liltingly softer. "And here, Angel I want you to think about what bothers you; that one thing about the 'Paper Heart Spirit' that you'd like to say something about, you know?" *

"Okay." Angel replies, "I think I understand." *

Princess starts swaying back and forth as she continues, "and now, in your mind, give the reason why you feel bothered, whatever it is or was, and then put that 'unhealthy' energy that was created," Princess pauses before continuing, "and I want you to put that energy into a song." *

"What?" Angel asks. "You want me to sing?" *

"Yes," Princess answers perceptively. "Sing to the imaginary 'Paper Heart Spirit' in front of you as if you're singing to the one that you imagine you might have feeling for; the one that is messing up your teenage vibes and disturbing the natural universe; your universe." *

"I Can Try." Angel says softly. She looks away for a moment then faces her imaginary 'Paper Heart Spirit' swaying dreamlike, Angel looks forward at the imaginary 'Paper Heart Spirit' that has turned into the image of the boy from school and he is looking back at her, and she sings, '**Are You Really My Friend**'

30

Are You Really My Friend

I think we will always be close
But there's times when you seem so distant
I wonder who you are and where you go
And where are you when I need you
When I'm lost, looking over the end
I think, what happened to what we had
And are you really my friend

When we first met last year in the school yard
We clicked and we had fun along the way
And in the classes that we had together
We helped each other to get through the day
But after what happened yesterday
What kind of message did you send
Do you just like me only sometimes
And are you really my friend

When you left with Sam to go to the playground
Did you even think about how I might feel
And now it's so awkward being left here by myself
And I don't want to be a third wheel

But you know, sometimes communicating can get difficult
And it's can be hard to do things on your own
But when we would take care of each other
It was kind a like we were not here all alone
So where will you be tomorrow
As new trouble comes around the bend
Will you be there for me when I need you
And are you really my friend

*Angel sings to the boy that she wants to know better, and imagines that the composed face of the boy is rather noncommittal. She needs to know if he is faithful to her or if she is just one of many others that he is involved with; that he is toying with as she questions, a mixture of anxious hope fills her countenance as the final words leave her lips and Angel then begins to dance freestyle; a mixture of waltz and ballet, swaying and moving to the plucking of the Japanese strings; her face reflecting a mixture of the uncertain conflict in her heart and a faint, far-off glint of hope that, as she circles round grows stronger and as the music slowly ends, she sets down on the ground, ever so gently and slowly raises her hands from her center to flow to the outside of her frame on both sides like a blooming flower and she smiles softly,... sadly. *

31

ACT ONE - SCENE THIRTEEN

ACT ONE — SCENE THIRTEEN:

The Players:
ANGEL, PRINCESS, GLADSTONE, FAITH, HOOT, SCROUNGE, BOBBY, JEROME & PRIVATE

THE TENT CIRCLE: Scrounge returns to the Circle calling out, "Angel,... Angel,... I got some,..." Scrounge rifles through both front pockets of her pea coat, pulls out an apple in each hand. "Some good really ones here." *

Angel steps over and receives the treasures from her mom. She grips one of the apples firmly in her hand and says, "Just the way I like em,..." *

"She don't like mushy apples." Scrounge says turning to Princess. "I had to go to the captain to get em." *

Angel goes to her tent and sits in front as she starts eating an apple. "Burrr." She says, shivering as she reaches into the tent to grab a wool sweater. "It's gonna be a cold night." *

"But it's gonna be clear and starry." Faith responds, as she looks at a weather report on her cell phone. "Fitting for out departure tomorrow." *

"Tomorrow." Hoot replies anxiously. "I still got so much to do to get ready for the big move." *

"You mean we." Faith corrects, not looking up from her phone. "*We* still got so much to do." *

"As usual," Hoot says smiling, "I stand corrected." Hoot steps into their tent to find everything has already been organized and semi packed. "Faith," he questions melodically, "What did you do?" *

"I just straightened things up a bit," Faith answers. "That's all." She looks up from her phone and smiles. "You were busy and I had a little bit of time,..." *

"You are so lucky." Gladstone says, peering into Hoot's tent. "You could send her over to my place to straighten things up anytime... I wouldn't mind." *

"You get your own girl." Hoot says with a comical concerned grin. "This one's mine." Hoot steps over to where Faith is sitting, looking into her phone, and he bends down and kisses her cheek softly. Faith looks up smiling and she and Hoot kiss. *

"Where are you at with your packing?" Princess asks Gladstone. "Can I look in your tent?" Princess moves toward Gladstone's tent. *

"No, no, no." Gladstone says, moving quickly to intercept Princess. Gladstone barricades the opening, waves one arm and says, "I don't think I'm ready for you to see how sloppy I can be." He zips the tent fly shut calls out, "Hoot? Faith? With everything happening so fast, I'm sure this has to have been weighing heavy on her mind, but Princess is now more than homeless. She's..." Gladstone searches for the right words, "She's gonna need to have someplace to sleep tonight; I was wondering..." *

"She's got a place to sleep in our tent." Faith interjects, "If she wants." *

Princess's face lights up. "I was kind a wondering what I was gonna do." Princess admits shyly. *

"And Hoot," Faith says nonchalantly, "You'll be bunking down in Gladstone's tent tonight." *

"What?" Hoot replies with fake concern in his tone. "But,..." *

"Princess," Faith says, concerned. "Any chance we could go get some of your stuff from your car?" *

Princess looks scared as she answers, "I,... I don't think so." She smiles nervously. "They're probably out there, watching and waiting for me to show back up." *

"I could go." Gladstone spouts. "I did tell them I was gonna buy the car anyway." *

"These are no nice people, Gladstone." Jerome reports. "If they get their hands on you, you may just end up disappearing." Jerome smiles. "But if you're in for a covert operation, I'm in." *

Faith quickly goes in and out of her tent. "Here;" She says, as she hands a sweatshirt to Princess. "Put this on. It's gonna be a cold night and you are hardly dressed for winter." Faith turns to Gladstone and Jerome and says, "Could you boys please just stay close tonight. We'll check out her car tomorrow, in the daylight, if it's still there." *

"Thank you." Princess Replies amiably. "I agree. I don't want anyone to get hurt. Anyways, I'm not really that worried; I know my brother wouldn't want me to be in danger because of his car." *

Bobby steps up and says, "Hey, I just heard that the city said something like, you know, if we clean up everything around all the tents, they'll let us stay here after all." *

"Really?" Jerome questions doubtfully. "And where did this information get disseminated from?" *

"Disseminated." Faith parrots happily. "That's a fifty-cent word, Jerome; used in the right context too." *

"Thank you, Ma'am." Jerome replies, turning back to Bobby. "So,...?" *

"So, it was some men in suits." Bobby replies. "They said they was from the City Counsel." *

"Hey man," Jerome spouts. "Anybody else here kind a feel like it's some bogus stratagem to build up hope and to inevitably get us to do the work that they're gonna end up having to do tomorrow, man?" *

"Stratagem?" Faith says, merrily. "Jerome, you're on a roll tonight. Do you do crossword puzzles?" *

"No, Ma'am." Jerome replies, "I started reading secret meanings in the puzzles and I was seeing encrypted algorithms in the numbered vertical and horizontal questions and answers. I mean, I'm not a cryptographer but after M-Theory and 'Nine Eleven' that stuff freaked me out." *

"Algorithms?" Faith says curiously. "Cryptographer? Them's all good words." *

"Them's?" Hoot replies looking over at Faith knowingly. *

Faith smiles back defiantly and says, "It's a plural of them." *

"The word them is already plural." Hoot says dismissively. He turns around and says with a confused look on his face, "And Jerome? What's, the M-Theory?" *

Jerome looks at Hoot incredulously and says, "M-theory is an idea about the basic substance of the universe. It's the leading runner for a universal "Theory of Everything" or, the big, T.O.E. that unifies power forces, like gravity with all other known power forces such as electromagnetism as well as some power forces that we don't know about yet." *

"I thought you said you didn't believe in gravity." Gladstone interrupts. "And, come on, the big toe?" *

"I don't believe in gravity." Jerome retorts. "Leastwise not in the way you do." He turns to Hoot and says, "Simply put, M-theory unifies quantum mechanics with relativity's gravitational force, and the force is a fundamental expression of some physical occurrence, like, time and distance; and power is defined as the amount of energy consumed per unit of time, like,… uh, the rate at which the "work" is done, and the work happens when there is some force that is causing the movement of an object." *

"You're way out there again, Jerome." Private interjects. He looks down at his dog and says, "He's So,… so far out there, man." Dumpster looks back at Private with renewed interest. *

"You never cease to amaze me Jerome." Hoot says with admiration. "You go from disseminating,…" *

"Disseminating?" Faith says inquiringly. "Hoot, where'd that word come from?" *

Hoot looks at Faith dismissively and mouths the words, "from you," before turning back to Jerome and continuing, "You go from disseminating life facts and figures to ambiguous and sometimes, unintelligible specifics, to your hand-picked collection of obscure conspiracy theories, to some curious quantum physics and scientific data. I'm amazed at the stuff that you put and retain inside your brain; like, electrons bouncing around the nucleus of your grey matter." *

"Like," Private says, "Far out, man. Far out indeed." *

Jerome smiles and says, "Sometimes I even amaze myself." *

"Hoot?" Faith says as she stands up, "I'm gonna go to the little store and get us some aspirin." *

"Just a minute," Hoot says standing up. "I'll go with you. It's getting dark and,..." *

"I'll go with her." Bobby interjects. "I need to get me some girl stuff anyway." She turns to Private and asks, "Can I take Dumpster with us? I'd feel a lot safer." *

Private looks down at Dumpster and asks, "You want to accompany these gypsies? It might be a perilous journey?" Dumpster sits up excitedly. "Guess he wants to go." Private says, smiling. *

As Hoot watches Faith, Bobby and Dumpster leave, Hoot mumbles under his breath, "Us,..." *

"What?" Private asks. "What did you say?" *

"Nothing,..." Hoot begins before saying, "She said she's going to the store and get us some aspirin." *

"Yeah, so?" Private quizzes. *

"Well," Hoot continues, "She's going to the store to get *me* some aspirin. She doesn't even take aspirin; she takes Tylenol; aspirin doesn't agree with her stomach." *

"So?" Private presses, "She's just taking good care of you, Hoot. That's a good thing." *

"Yeah," Hoot agrees, looking off and away with a slight smile and says softly, "that's a good thing." Hoot watches his wife and Bobby disappear down the sidewalk before turning back to the others on the Circle and then says, "Yeah, she takes care of me." *

Hoot pulls out a harmonica and plays some notes before he sings, **'She Takes Care Of Me'**

32

ACT ONE - SCENE FOURTEEN

ACT ONE — SCENE FOURTEEN:

The Players:
PRINCESS, JEROME, PRIVATE GLADSTONE & HOOT

THE TENT CIRCLE: It is a cold, starry night. Most everyone is out picking up garbage with a slim, but unlikely hope that they will not have to move the following morning. Most everyone that is, except Scrounge, who is sitting in a camping chair just outside her tent, pretending that she doesn't notice the others working. *

Princess joins the others around and about the Circle and has a trash bag in one hand and while selectively picking up garbage and litter in the darkness with a plastic glove on, she says, "This doesn't seem right." *

"What do you mean?" Gladstone asks. "It's not the city's trash; we put it here." *

"Isn't there some other way to solve homelessness," Princess continues, "besides kicking people out of one place only to move some of them somewhere else a block or two away? And what about the other people that don't get a space at the new spot? What about them? Is this happening everywhere?" *

"Get used to it honey," Scrounge interjects from within her chair, "ain't nobody caring no more bout us." *

"That can't be true." Princess contradicts. "This is a big problem, but,..." *

"Half of all homelessness is in one of five states." Jerome replies from within the darkness of tents behind the Circle. "California, New York, Florida, Texas and here in Washington State; the three *cities* that have the most homeless people are, New York, LA and Seattle." *

"Well if they know that," Princess replies, "can't the government concentrate on those cities?" *

"Not that easy." Jerome answers, stepping out of the shadows. "Accounting tricks make it hard to know if U.S. homelessness has increased or decreased. The government has shifted from offering the homeless a room in temporary housing to offering assistance to people to defray the cost of moving into and renting a private home; they don't count most of those in New York's rapid re-housing as homeless, even though there's no guarantee they'll have a place from month to month." *

"You're just full of statistics, aren't you?" Scrounge quips. *

"Hey, why are you just sitting there?" Jerome says to Scrounge. "We could use some help here." *

"Ain't my junk." Scrounge replies. *

"Lame, Scrounge." Gladstone interjects. "I'm picking up a lot of stuff that ain't mine." *

"Well, thank you for that." Scrounge replies. "Back to Jerome, where do you get all this information?" *

"I read a lot from my phone." Jerome answers as he bends over to pick up some trash. "And I ingest it all with a notion of disbelief and a touch of dubious doubt, but I do fact checking by info-roaming." *

"Not to mention," Hoot interjects, "Jerome has total recall; he remembers everything he reads." *

"Is that true?" Princess asks astonished. "I sure could a used that when I was in school." *

"Didn't help me much." Jerome answers. "I was always in trouble and I got expelled." *

"What did you do to get kicked out of school?" Faith asks. *

"I was just smarter than everyone else and I knew it." Jerome replies, his voice coming from a distance and muffled because he is bending over to pick up trash. "But there was this one teacher that didn't like me," Jerome's voice becomes clearer as he stands up. "He thought I was cheating all the time. He kept looking for the methods I was using to cheat on his tests." Jerome laughs.

"That's terrible." Faith responds with concern. *

"One time," Jerome continues, "I was put in this closet where they had this collection of left-over Civil Defense rations, you know, in case they dropped the bomb or something? Anyway, it was dark and I had to take the test by the thin light coming through the crack in the door." He laughs again. "I answered all the questions before the rest of the class and answered almost all the questions right. So he took me to the principal's office and said I had cheated on the test. I asked to take the test over again to prove I knew the material, but they didn't care. I think they wanted some reason to get me out of there." *

"Why would they do that?" Princess asks. *

"I was kind of a smart aleck," Jerome answers. "Rubbed a lot of teachers the wrong way." *

"That'll do it." Hoot replies. *

Jerome smiles at Princess and asks, "You want some more statistics? How about this one? African Americans represent 13% of the U.S. population but almost half of all people experiencing homelessness are African Americans, and over half of the individuals who are homeless with children are African Americans." *

"That's terrible." Princess replies with concern. *

"Well how about this," Jerome says, looking at Private, "38,000 veterans face homelessness on any given night. And," Jerome looks at Gladstone. "Males are more likely than women to be homeless in the U.S. And," Jerome looks but doesn't find Angel before saying, "About 700,000 kids under 18 without a parent or guardian experience homelessness each year. And," Jerome looks over at Hoot and Faith who with Bobby and Dumpster, have arrived back from the store. "Since 2007 the number of beds provided for homeless people in transitional housing which provides support to successfully move the homeless to permanent housing has been cut in half." *

Dumpster goes over to Private and sits down next to him. Private looks down and asks, "Did they get you anything special?" Dumpster looks back happily. Private, with concern on his face, says, "Well, I hope they paid for it this time." *

"That was just a mistake and you know it." Bobby barks back mildly annoyed. *

"So you say," Private says doubtfully, "So you say." *

"Why is it that the government doesn't care anymore?" Princess asks. "That's terrible." *

"That's harsh." Jerome answers. "But not totally accurate. It really depends on how you're classified. For instance, an individual is classified or considered to be chronically homeless if, that he or she, has a disability, including a substance use disorder, post-traumatic stress disorder and or a serious mental illness and has been homeless continuously for at least a year or on at least four occasions in the last three years. And so, it's been generally calculated that each night, nearly a quarter of the homeless population is considered chronically homeless." *

"My wariness to all of these facts," Faith says, "leaves me feeling hollow." *

"This all seems so hopeless, you know?" Princess says, "Is there no hope?" *

"Homelessness," Jerome says, "has been exacerbated by the nation's lack of affordable housing." *

"Exacerbated?" Faith parrots. "Do you even know how to spell that word?" *

Jerome smiles at Faith before continuing, "From the little censuses being taken by the city or the state or for that matter, the federal government, it's hard to be accurate about how big the problem really is, but yes, there are some possible solutions; it's possible for instance that housing deregulation could wipe out the majority of homelessness in San Francisco. Homelessness would fall by 54 percent in San Francisco, 40 percent in Los Angeles, and 23 percent in New York City. And it would reduce homelessness overall by an average of 31 percent." Jerome looks annoyed as he glances over at Scrounge. "Hey, you gonna help us here? Lot of the garbage Princess is picking up is, I believe, yours." *

"I don't lay claim on any of it." Scrounge replies. "And why don't you mind your own business?" *

"Because," Jerome presses, "This is all of our business in the Circle, and you're part of it." *

Scrounge looks around slightly and says, "Hmm, no. I ain't feeling it. Looks like work and I ain't believing that they're changing their mind for what they're gonna do tomorrow morning. I ain't about to be doing their work when they're gonna kick us off this land anyway." *

Scrounge gets out of her chair, and standing up, she looks all around before, unapologetically she sings, **'Mr. Lazy Bones'**

33

Mr. Lazy Bones

If I have to, I guess I can do it
But, I'm still gonna wait for a moment to see
Whether someone else is gonna step in and end up doing
That whatever that was intended for me
I'm not feeling the slightest of guilt
Schluffing things off like your neighborhood jerk
Just as long as I can continue avoiding having to do
What seems like too much work
Oh, notwithstanding the proverbial sticks and stones
They say what they will but I'm still taking it easy
I'm Mr. lazy bones

There they are, running around to get their things done
Admittedly there's a lot going on
But why would they like to include me for their own sakes
To expect I'd just follow along
Mm, I'm going down that path of least resistance

I'm ignoring any guilty conscience call
And I'm looking to have a little more time to myself
And hopefully end up doing nothing at all
I see them talking over there
with their less-than subtle whispers and groans
But I'm ain't listening to what any of them have to say
I'm Mr. lazy bones

I hold no malice for anyone or anything
As long as they just leave me alone
I'm saving myself, my strength and get-up-and-go
So please don't pull me out and away from my home,... Yeah
I'm easing myself back into the shadows
To see what'll happen when time slips away
There's always that someone who gets tired of waiting
And will step up to do the work, to save the day
And I know I lack a sense of decorum
Most folks are feeling that it's really not fair
They're only gonna end up frustrating themselves
Because, well I really don't care
Oh, I got better things to do with my life
then being taken out of my comfort zones
So, maybe later if I'm feeling it but otherwise, come on
I'm Mr. lazy bones

Oh, I see them talking over there to themselves
In their angry and frustrated tones
But I can't hear em anymore
Cause I'm walking the other way
I'm Mr. Lazy bones

34

END OF ACT ONE

END

OF

ACT ONE

'RESILIENT'
A (WEB-BASED EPISODIC)
MUSICAL PLAY & STORY
ACT TWO

Screenplay:
LORD CHESTER L. BALDWIN II

Music
LORD BALDWIN

Lyrics
LORD BALDWIN
(LORD CHESTER L. BALDWIN II)

Except: **"Are You Really My Friend"**

Lyrics
Tabby (Ruby) Bastion Baldwin & Lord Baldwin

Editing & Suggestions
Elizabeth Baldwin
&
Meridith Anne Baldwin

35

List of Music and Songs for ACT TWO

List of Music and Songs
and the Performers
for ACT 2

Planet Z
 INTERLUDE MUSIC   ACT TWO, SCENE ONE

My Best Friend
 FAITH *   ACT TWO, SCENE THREE

Looking Like The Enemy
 BOBBY *   ACT TWO, SCENE FOUR

I'll Make A Space For You
 GLADSTONE *   ACT TWO, SCENE FIVE

36

ACT TWO - SCENE ONE

ACT TWO — SCENE ONE:

PLANET Z

The Players:
HOOT, GLADSTONE, JEROME, SCROUNGE,
FAITH, PRIVATE, ANGEL & BOBBY

SEMICIRCLE OF TENTS: There's a semicircle of tents with people sitting motionless in a semicircle in front of the tents. After the music, (Planet Z) begins, everyone suddenly goes into motion, with each person pantomiming their particular routine.

HOOT (in 4/4 time) is writing words to a song on a piece of paper and then picks up the 'Guitar with No Strings' and strums it while looking at the lyrics before putting the 'Guitar with No Strings' back down and goes back to writing the lyrics,...

JEROME (in 3/4 time) looks suspiciously from the left, then to the right like he's being watched, then pulls something out from his pocket and looks carefully at the contents before putting it back into his pocket and looks suspiciously from the left, then to the right like he's being watched,...

FAITH (in 8/4 time) appears to be using a cell phone doing genealogy and then stops and writes something down, then she looks back and forth between her documentation and her cell phone then sets the documentation down and begins to use the cell phone again to doing genealogy,...

SCROUNGE (in 6/3 time) with her head moving from side to side, she is looking in the alleyways between the tents for some treasure and then spies something and picks it up only to examine it before throwing it away and with her head moving from side to side is looking she is looking in the alleyways between the tents for some treasure,...

PRIVATE (in 4/4 time) stands up at attention, looks around and after he perceives that no one is there, he sits back down and buries his head in his hands and then again, stands back up at attention and looks around,...

GLADSTONE (in 2/4 time) already standing, bows vaguely with his head slightly tilted as he slowly flies his left hand in a waving motion from right to left, then slowly flies his right hand in a waving motion from left to right, then sits, tilts his head to the left as he scratches the right side of his head with his right hand, then he stands, bows vaguely with his head slightly tilted as he slowly flies his left hand in a waving motion from right to left, then slowly flies his right hand in a waving motion from left to right,...

ANGEL (in 3/4 time) with pointe shoes rises from the floor, 'does a plie' then a releve' while standing on her toes, then does a Pirouette, sits, then rises from the floor repeating the process,...

BOBBY (in free time) already standing, puts her arms down and out from her side like she is in a boxing ring holding the ropes from one of the corners, then, like an imaginary bell rang, she moves forward, shadow boxing, using the *short* method, moving her head and body to the left and right, constantly slipping punches and moving in for the closer body shots, then hearing the imaginary bell again, she goes back to her corner, puts her arms out like she is in a boxing ring holding the ropes from one of the corners,... then, like an imaginary bell rang, she moves forward, shadow boxing,...

As the music begins playing, everyone is frozen in their starting positions.

For this piece we imagine that all of these people are stuck in a time loop where they repetitiously go through the motions of their given parts; each break implies that each set is another day coming and going by and that each of these players are all stuck in their same routines, trapped in their own time loop and destined to have to repeat themselves over and over.

First Movement:
After 25 seconds, (beginning at :25) they all begin at the same time and are in motion for 30 seconds (ending at :55) before each ends their part; each ending at the same time.

Second Movement:

20 seconds later, (thus beginning at 1:15), they all begin again at the same time and are in motion for another 25 seconds, (thus ending at 1:40).

Third Movement:

20 seconds later, (thus beginning at 1:55), they all begin again at the same time and are again in motion for another 25 seconds, but 15 seconds after they begin, (at 2:10) **PRINCESS** arrives and astonished by what she sees, she walks over and gently touches **FAITH** to wake her up. That is to say, she breaks **FAITH** out of her routine. **FAITH** stands up and looks around, confounded at seeing everyone else in their routines. 15 seconds later, (at 2:20) **FAITH** wakes up **HOOT** by physically embracing him and giving him a kiss. After **HOOT** looks around, they both watch as everyone else finishes their routines, (thus ending at 2:25).

Fourth Movement:

20 seconds later, (beginning at 2:40), they all begin again at the same time and are again in motion for another 25 seconds, but 5 seconds after they begin, (at 2:45) **HOOT** wakes up **GLADSTONE** and breaks him out of his routine. 15 seconds after that, (at 3:00), **FAITH** wakes up **ANGEL** and breaks her out of her routine. A few seconds after that, (at about 3:05), **ANGEL** wakes up her mother **SCROUNGE** and breaks her out of her routine just in time to see everyone else finishing their routines and returning to their starting positions, (thus ending at 3:10).

Fifth Movement:

20 seconds later, (beginning at 3:25), **PRIVATE** and **BOBBY** are again in motion, but 5 seconds after they begin, (at 3:30) **GLADSTONE** wakes up **JEROME** to break him out of his routine but **JEROME** has a hard time letting his routine go. Meanwhile,

SCROUNGE is mesmerized watching **PRIVATE** and **BOBBY** doing their routine and begins to do her routine again but she is woken back up again by **FAITH** who instructs her with hand motions to look away. At 3:40, **HOOT** wakes up **PRIVATE**, breaking him out of his routine and 10 seconds later, (at 3:50) **ANGEL** wakes up **BOBBY** and breaks her out of her routine.

Sixth Movement:

It is 3:58 and with everyone now conscious, they each look to each other with confusion, not knowing exactly what to do next. As the music is coming to a close, we see **JEROME** and **SCROUNGE** still struggling to fight off the urge to not do their routine. **JEROME** looks suspiciously from the left to the right but then breaks out of the routine and joins the others. **SCROUNGE** spies something and reaches down to pick it up but then breaks out for a moment only to see something again and is drawn to it but as she reaches down, **ANGEL** pulls at **SCROUNGE'S** arm, which breaks **SCROUNGE** out of the trance. Meanwhile, **FAITH** points out the fourth wall at the audience and everyone looks out with her in astonishment. The music fades, the curtain closes.

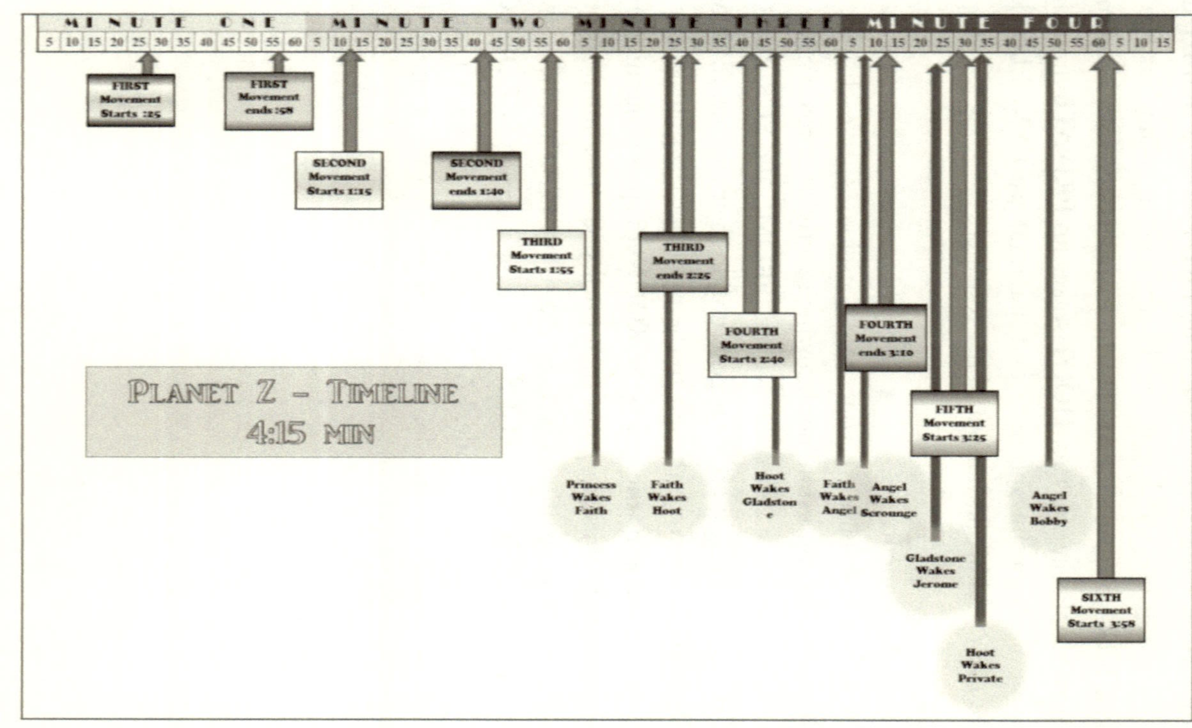
MINUTE ONE
MINUTE TWO
MINUTE THREE
MINUTE FOUR
5 10 15 20 25 30 35 40 45 50 55 60 5 10 15 20 25 30 35 40 45 50 55 60 5 10 15 20 25 30 35 40 45 50 55 60 5 10 15 20 25 30 35 40 45 50 55 60 5 10 15
PLANET Z – TIMELINE
4:15 MIN
FIRST Movement Starts :25
FIRST Movement ends :58
SECOND Movement Starts 1:15
SECOND Movement ends 1:40
THIRD Movement Starts 1:55
THIRD Movement ends 2:25
FOURTH Movement Starts 2:40
FOURTH Movement ends 3:10
FIFTH Movement Starts 3:25
SIXTH Movement Starts 3:58
Princess Wakes Faith
Faith Wakes Hoot
Hoot Wakes Gladstone
Faith Wakes Angel
Angel Wakes Scrounge
Gladstone Wakes Jerome
Hoot Wakes Private
Angel Wakes Bobby

37

ACT TWO - SCENE TWO

ACT TWO — SCENE TWO:

Players:

JEROME, PRIVATE, ROGER & DUMPSTER

EXT — DEEP INSIDE THE TENT CAMP: Jerome and Private are heading to the wall where two Porta Potties sit on a pallet platform. As they approach, they find that there is a line waiting to use the facilities. "What's going on?" Jerome asks. *

As they get closer, they see Roger, standing in front of the line, calling out to the folks in the line. "We are now managing these facilities." Roger says, flanked by two of his cronies. "And anyone wanting to use em will need to pay us fifty cents." There is a soft groaning from some of the people in the line and an even louder amount of voices of complaining, causing Roger to smile as he repeats, "only fifty cents." *

"They can't do that." Jerome says, disgruntled. *

"This is the last night." Private says calmly. "He's just cashing in, one last time on everyone else's misery and sorrow. It's all a guy like him knows how to get on in his sorry life." *

"Well," Jerome says annoyed, "I'm not gonna stand for this,..." *

"Yes, you are, man." Private says sternly, as he puts his arm out to stop Jerome from moving forward. Dumpster growls softly and Private looks down and says, "Stop that. This is Jerome; he's my friend." *

"Good thing too." Jerome replies heatedly. *

"You know?" Private declares softly, "For a guy as smart as you, sometimes you can be downright stupid." Private glances about before saying knowingly, "If you look real close," Private nods his head. "You'll notice that one of Roger's friends there, on the left?" *

Jerome nods understandingly. *

"He's got a knife in his hand." Private gives Jerome a slight Vulcan grip before saying, "You see there? That small bulge in the front of Roger's waist" under his shirt there?" *

"Yeah?" Jerome answers slowly. *

"That's probably a gun." Private replies. *

"But he shouldn't be able to do this." Jerome complains. *

Private declares kindly, "You're not hearing me, Jerome. He's like the city council; with that gun, he's holding all the cards. I know you're not stupid. You remember Sun Tzu?" *

"Art of War." Jerome answers, "Chinese military strategist." *

"Right." Private replies. "So, you know, ya gotta know how and when to pick your battles." With a weighted tone, Private continues, "and this ain't worth getting hurt for. Come on," Private says tugging Dumpster's leash, "let's go to the Mission." *

As they leave the line and start for the Mission, Roger sees them leaving and he calls out, "Sorry boys, business is booming tonight." He frowns. "But we didn't want your business anyway." *

Jerome turns and stops to say something but with Private quickly yanking him away, Jerome is cut short. Dumpster growls again but this time with his face looking directly at Roger, who pretends he's not scared. *

A block later, Private stops and facing Jerome, says, "You want to get us both killed?" *

"What do you mean?" Jerome returns. *

"Do you see things?" Private, asks, looking sternly, "I mean, did you really see his eyes? Did you see where his hand went straight for as soon as you stopped?" *

"No." answers Jerome, looking bewildered. *

"If Dumpster here hadn't freaked him out, we'd a been in

trouble." Private looks down at Dumpster and smiles before continuing, "Roger's flying high *and* packing, man." Private says less hardheartedly. "That's a dangerous combination in itself, man. But that guy has got a few screws loose too, not to mention," Private makes a disbelieving face and says, "you humiliated him in front of his crew this afternoon." *

"He's such an idiot." Jerome spouts, waving his hands in the air. *

Well idiot or not," Private returns, "he's got it in for you. And,..." Private, with Dumpster by his side, starts walking with Jerome and Private says delicately, "in his state right now, he has a short fuse." *

"I get it." Jerome counters, "We're in the real world, here." He grimaces, "So, we just walk away?" *

"Yeah, we walk away." Private says as they cross the street. "We walk away and we live." *

"But is it fair that,...?" Jerome begins. *

"Fair?" Private parrots, looking angry. "Ain't no fair. But I don't want us to be the reason Roger tries to shoot you and ends up shooting and killing somebody in that line that need to take a leak. You know what I'm saying here? It leads back to what I told you before." *

"What you told me?" Jerome asks, confused. "How long ago, man?" *

"Ya gotta know how and when to pick your battles." Private says incredulously. He stops suddenly in front of Jerome and stops, looking him face to face, "And that?" Private puts up a raised hand as if to say stop and says, "that was *not* the time." *

38

ACT TWO - SCENE THREE

ACT TWO — SCENE THREE:

The Players:
FAITH, HOOT, PRINCESS, GLADSTONE, JEROME,
PRIVATE, BOBBY, SCROUNGE & ANGEL

THE TENT CIRCLE: Private and Jerome return from the Mission and they step over to Bobby's tent and Private calls out, "Hey Bobby, you okay?" Dumpster sees a small hole in the bottom of the tent zipper and goes in. *

"Yeah I'm fine." Bobby answers dismissively, then yells, "Dumpster, what are you doing here?" *

"Sorry," Private apologizes, "Can I come in and get him?" *

Bobby is laughing for a brief moment then answers, "Yes. Get your dumb dog outta here." *

"What's going on?" Hoot asks, stepping over to Bobby's tent. *

Private steps in close to Hoot and says, softly, "She got freaked out at the Mission. Thought it was Immigration and Customs folks." *

"Was it?" Hoot asks. *

"No," Private answers, "Just some suits from the city spying on how things are going here." Private opens the zipper and reaches in to Bobby's tent and grabs Dumpster's collar. He drags the dog from the tent and zips the tent shut saying, "Sorry Bobby." Private says as he kneels down and looks Dumpster in the eyes, smiling knowingly, asks loudly, "Now how did you get off your leash?" *

"I can only guess." Bobby answers sarcastically from inside her tent. *

"Well it's good that she has someone like you," Hoot replies with concern, as he and Private begin walking away from Bobby's tent. Hoot stops, looks Private in the face and says, "It's good that she has someone like you to be her friend and to look after her." *

"Well, yeah, I guess." Private says reflectively. *

Private turns back in the direction of Bobby's tent and says, "If you need anything, just let me know." *

"I'm okay, I'm okay." Bobby answers wryly. "I just need some time to get my stuff together." *

"Did you take your aspirin yet?" Faith asks from within her tent. *

"Really woman?" Hoot answers, standing close to the street, "You can be such a pesterer at times." *

"Pesterer or not," Faith responds, peeking out of the tent, "Did you take your aspirin yet?" *

"Yes, yes woman," Hoot replies, "I did, in fact, take the stupid aspirin a while ago." *

"That's good." Faith replies as she goes back in her tent. "Did you take your other medicine too?" Faith asks from within the tent again. *

"Yes dear." Hoot replies sarcastically. "And I drank all the water I was supposed to." *

"That's nice." Faith's voice responds from within. "I love you." *

After a long pause of silence Faith's voice calls out softly, "Well?" *

"Well what?" Hoot responds. *

"Well if you don't know,..." Faith's voice calls out nonchalantly. *

"Okay, okay." Hoot says with a note of annoyance. "I love you too." *

After another pause of silence Faith says melodiously, "Now that wasn't so hard, was it?" *

Hoot grunts to himself but a smile flashes across his face. *

"You two really have something going, don't you?" Princess says to Hoot. *

"Yeah, I guess." Hoot answers as he sits down in a camp chair outside his tent. *

"You guess?" Faith's voice calls out from within the tent. *

"Woman, she was talking to me." Hoot replies & turns to Princess. "You were talking to me, right?" *

Princess looks nervous as she answers, "I don't want to get anyone,..." *

"You're not getting anyone in trouble here." Faith responds, coming out of the tent. "This man here," Faith points to Hoot, "just gets a little bit too comfortable at times and I gotta shake things up a bit so he remembers what that special thing we have, is." *

"Special thing?" Hoot replies smiling. "Is that what we're calling our relationship? Special thing?" *

"You just stop this right now, mister." Faith says, jokingly. "You know what I'm talking about." *

Hoot steps over to Faith and unexpectedly grabs her by the

waist, pulls her in close and with them face to face, Hoot says with a smile, "Is this, part of that special thing you're talking about?" *

Faith struggles and pulls herself loose, regains her composure, smiles back and says, "You behave." *

"I can't help it." Hoot says with a knowing grin; looking away from Faith as he waves his arms about, "The woman's crazy about me." *

"Crazy?" Faith parrots questioningly, then smiles and says, "well, maybe." *

Faith turns to Princess, then looks over at Hoot as she lovingly sings, **'My Best Friend'**

As the song begins, Bobby comes out of her tent, followed by Jerome, then Angel and finally, Scrounge. Hoot stands, looks back at Faith with a kind of amazement as she sings this song, knowing that in the past, Faith has never been so bold as to put herself out there in such a fashion, singing a song and moreover, in front of these other people. Faith smiles knowingly to Hoot through the song,

39

My Best Friend

Going through life finding the right footing to be sure
Is a difficult task, especially if you're going it alone.
So it's nice to have a fellow comrade to go with me on the tour
of the many travelings we face on our way back home.
And there you are, your laughter's dancing inside my mind
must a been knowing full-well it's just what I need;
and there you go, ministering with your own brand of kind
aimed directly to bring out the best in me.
We are free to grow separately yet without ever growing apart
You're with me from the start,
And now you're here with me to the end, yeah;
you are the fuel for the flame that burns inside my heart
You; my best friend.
Hard to remember a time when you weren't there
Seems we've always been as one, together somehow.
We have our special ways; striving to be just and fair
So ready to champion all the good that life and love will allow.

And there you are with that smile and the sparkle in your eyes
Knowing full-well, it is just what I need.
And there's nobody I'd rather be with, and oh, it'll be nice
to have you in my life for eternity.
Here we are, moving on down the path to some unknown part
You're being with me sure has been a Godsend, yeah;
You are the fuel for the flame that burns inside my heart
You; my best friend.

There is a guitar solo by Hoot in the middle of the song between the two verses as well as in closing after Faith has finished singing the song. During those times, Hoot picks up the 'Guitar with No Strings' and, while smiling back at Faith, Hoot plays the two lead guitar riffs, first, as a prelude to the second verse and second, to end the song. Hoot sets down the 'Guitar with No Strings' gently pulls Faith in close and passionately kisses her. *

7

40

ACT TWO - SCENE FOUR

The Players:
HOOT, BOBBY, PRIVATE, JEROME, PRINCESS,
GLADSTONE, FAITH, SCROUNGE & ANGEL

THE TENT CIRCLE: Seeing Bobby out of her tent, sporting blue boxing gloves, wearing a black corners jacket, red boxing trunks, blue and black boxing shoes and a grey-knit beanie, Hoot steps over and says, "Getting ready to do some damage?" *

"Thinking about it." Bobby replies as she tightens the vertical duffle bag into position. *

Heard what happened." Hoot says. "Gotta be a bummer having to always be looking over your shoulder for some bad guy." *

"Yeah, I do get tired of it." Bobby answers, glancing over at

Private who is looking back over at her. She turns to Hoot and says pensively, "It gets old but I gotta always be on my guard." She turns and begins rabbit punching her punching bag. *

"Yeah, that really sucks." Hoot agrees. "But there's got to be some way to fix this." *

"Not unless you got a way," Bobby returns, "to get some legal paper that says I'm a U.S. Citizen." *

"You could change your name," Jerome spouts, "or get married to a U.S. Citizen and change your name, but if you're an undocumented immigrant, there's a lot of stuff you gotta go through and to be fair, with this xenophobic and prejudicially racist Trump administration, your chances are real slim and there's no telling what will happen." *

"But it is an option?" Private asks as he steps into the conversation. *

"Well,..." Jerome answers hesitatingly, "yeah, it's an option." Jerome turns to Bobby and says, "but for starters, undocumented immigrants don't have a legal path to citizenship and so, are unable to obtain a Social Security number. So even if you do get married, you can't legally work here." *

"Not very encouraging." Bobby says, continuing to punch her punching bag without looking up. *

"Well,..." Jerome says hesitatingly while drawing breath through his nose as he watches Bobby taking out her frustration on the bag, "the Bureau of Immigration laws were put into place in 1895, and right after that, the "Great Wave" happened from 1900 to 1920, where 24 million immigrants arrived. So, to control things, a new immigration policy was passed in 1921 where immigration was limited by assigning each nationality a quota based on its representation in the past U.S. census figures which favored immigrants from Northwestern Europe." *

"Well, that doesn't seem fair." Scrounge remarks. *

"No it doesn't." Bobby replies, giving the bag a hard, one-two. *

"Yeah," Jerome reports, "but it did do what they intended it to do; it slowed down immigration." *

"So, problem solved, right?" Hoot asks. *

"No, World War II happened," Jerome says, "that is to say, World War II was the catalyst for,…" *

"Catalyst." Faith parrots without looking up from her computer, "that's a good word." *

Jerome looks at Faith with incredulousness before saying, "during World War II the United States signed the Mexican Farm Labor Agreement with Mexico to help the war effort. It was called the Bracero Program and was intended to fill the labor shortage in agriculture because of the war and until 1964, the U.S. allowed hundreds of thousands of braceros in, per year." *

Bobby grunts as she hits the bag with all her strength, knocking it off its pallet platform. *

"Wow," Jerome chuckles, "Remind me to stay on your good side." *

"I ain't mad at you." Bobby says, out of breath. *

"Good thing." Jerome says as he helps Bobby put the bag in place on the pallet platform. "By the way," Jerome says, stepping off the platform, "the state of Texas was banned to be in the Bracero Program by the Mexican government because of the rampant and widespread hatred and discrimination by Texans for the Mexicans, including the lynching of Mexicans along the border." *

"Still going on today." Scrounge replies. "Except they use guns instead of ropes." *

"True that." Jerome replies. "but in 1965," Jerome turns his head to one side and scratches the back of his head, "Congress shifted the source countries of immigrants away from Europe. Then, right up to now, most applicants for immigration visas came from Asia and Latin America and immigrants went from 320,000 to over a million per year by the 21st century. So, the United States created a policy to control the admission of refugees and started limiting the number of immigration visas available each year, but the after-math of the Bracero Program was it left millions od undocumented Mexican scattered throughout the U.S." *

"And then things went crazy sideways with President Trump, right?" Gladstone replies. *

With the mention of Trump, Bobby violently attacks the bag, knocking it over again. *

"Yeah," Jerome answers, looking over at Bobby and Private resetting the bag, "Trump made immigration his campaign platform; to build a border wall and make Mexico pay for it." *

"Yeah," Bobby interjects as she temporarily stops hitting the bag. "And how did that turn out?" *

Jerome grins and shrugs his shoulder before continuing, "Trump also promised to deport all undocumented immigrants, to defund sanctuary cities, to ban any and all Muslims from entering the United States, to limit legal immigration, and to triple the number of ICE agents." *

Bobby grimaces with the mention of the ICE and goes back to punching the bag. *

"And, as you may remember," Jerome continues, now slightly shivering from the onset of a cold, slow breeze that permeates throughout the whole encampment, "Trump signed a travel ban restricting admission to over 135 million potential immigrants and nonimmigrant visitors from seven countries — Libya, Iran, Somalia, Syria, Yemen, North Korea and Venezuela." *

"So yeah," Bobby interjects, punching the bag. "I'm basically screwed. Can't work," She hits the bag. "Can't box;" She hits the bag. "I'm shunned by millions of Americans; people I grew up with and lived with." She hits the bag. "Worse yet," She stops to catch her breath and says with heavy breathing, "Even if I was an American citizen, I'm still hated by everyone in the red states." She turns and hits the bag. "And all because of my ethnicity." She says as she hits the bag repeatedly. *

"Not everyone, dear," Faith returns, looking up from her computer, "there's a lot of good people everywhere and in the red states; it's just that we are living in the last days and in a time where love is struggling to overcome the hate that abounds from the personification of evil." *

"Are you saying Trump is the devil?" Scrounge asks. "I ain't saying you're wrong." *

"No," Faith answers, "Trump is not *the* devil. Mostly he's a misguided person of low intelligence in the pursuit of worldly power and money, with little to no care about what happens to anyone else, including his own constituents and even his own family and friends." *

Bobby moves in close hitting the bag with quick, rapid fire punches. *.

Faith smiles knowingly at Bobby and says, "We've all seen that when people around Trump no longer serve a purpose towards his ends; when they stop feeding his already over-inflated ego, he fires them, alienates them, or casts them out of his life and with extreme, appalling, vindictive ferocity." *

"Ferocity?" Hoot questions, laughingly. "Constituents? A misguided person of low intelligence?" Hoot laughs louder, "You've really raised the bar here, honey." *

Bobby hits the bag with a couple short but powerful blows and after looking both ways, turns to everyone around her and starts singing, **'Looking Like The Enemy'**

4I

Looking Like The Enemy

There's no telling if things'll ever change;
us hurting each other, time and time again,
but for now, my big concern is to make it to tomorrow
where I'm not judged for the way I look to them.
And to them, I may look like I'm strong and wild,
and that's just the way I want it to be;
instead of them sensing a weakness to exploit
because I'm,... Looking like the enemy.

They say there is no separation here anymore;
there's no caste lives and that biased bigotry is gone.
And that is so easy to say if you're the privileged
or oblivious to what's really going on.
They can go where they want, see and do what they will,
and look with little more than a dull interest in me,
but I can't help the way things are right now
or the fact that I'm,... Looking like the enemy.

Stereotypes, prejudices, discrimination and such;
they fuel racism and hatred from another's past.
They don't know me, my passions; who I really am;
they only know of what they see standing in their path.

There's no telling if anything will ever change,
but here we're hurting each other because of some father's sin,
so for now my big hope is to get to a time and place
where I won't be judged for the color of my skin.
And to you, I might look like I'm the menace, a threat;
it's a real drag to be the one striped of dignity,
and I'm reduced to keeping a low profile, and in my own town?
It's all because I'm,... Looking like the enemy,...
Looking like the enemy.

As the singing stops, she moves her head and body to the left and right, slipping punches and moving in for closer body shots but suddenly she loses the gloves and evolves from her fighter's rhythm with the shuffling of her feet and the defensive rocking of her body back and forth, to a kind of artistic dance with light, graceful, fluid movements, filled with poise and elegance, like ballet, but with artistic freedom to move and sway as she feels her way, every now and then she reverts back to her shadowboxing, but now resolved with a new sense of determination and strength, she no longer feels the need to feel afraid and as she finds this new sense of freedom she looks over to Private with loving regard and an expression of renewed hope.

42

ACT TWO - SCENE FIVE

ACT TWO — SCENE FIVE:

The Players:
**GLADSTONE, PRINCESS, HOOT, FAITH, JEROME,
PRIVATE, BOBBY, SCROUNGE & ANGEL**

EXT. THE TENT CIRCLE: "It's gotten colder but everyone seems determined to stay up." Scrounge says to Angel. "But not me. I'm going to bed to get some sleep." Scrounge unzips the fly to the tent and says, "Tomorrow's gonna be a long day." *

"I'm not ready to go to bed yet." Angel replies, leaning in her mother's direction to get a kiss. When Scrounge does not take notice, Angel says, "Did you forget something?" *

"Uh, I don't know." Scrounge replies from within the tent. "Did I?" *

"Uh, no," Angel replies sheepishly. "No, you're fine." *

Bobby, Jerome and Private are sitting in foldable camping chairs around a propane heater that they call the fire, Hoot stands by the fire adjusting the valve knob to get more heat. *

Angel walks over and stands over Faith and Princess who are in front of Faith's tent, sitting on a folded wool blanket that sits over a camping pad mat that is the only insulation between them and the concrete of the parking lot. Wrapped around Faith and Princess is yet another wool blanket. *

"You guys look warm." Hoot says with a slight tone of jealousy. *

"We got more room here." Faith says. "You're welcome to join us; we can skootch over a bit." *

"Is skootch really a word?" Hoot asks disbelievingly. *

"Sure it is." Faith replies knowingly. "It means to move over a very small distance." *

"I'm okay." Hoot returns. "I think you'd have to move over more than a small distance to fit this big bottom of mine. Anyway, this fire, that is to say, the propane heater is,... warm." *

"Barely." Says Gladstone and he moves in a bit closer to it. "I think the tank is running out." *
"No," Hoot contradicts, "it's got fuel; it's just really cold out here tonight." *

"So Princess," Faith says, turning to Princess, "what are you gonna do after tomorrow morning?" *

"Not sure,..." Princess answers, glancing quickly over at Gladstone but half hoping he didn't see her. "When I was getting hot water at the CCC, someone invited me to go under the bridge." *

Gladstone, who was pretending not to be eavesdropping on the conversation, suddenly perks up and asks "Who was it that asked you? It wasn't Roger was it?" *

Pretending to be a little indignant but in truth, happy to be overheard, Princess replies, "I don't know who it was, but it wasn't Roger. You told me to stay away from him, so I did." *

Gladstone is decidedly embarrassed. He turns back around to the feel the propane heated fire and turns away from Princess's gaze. *

Faith smiles and silently motions for Angel to sit next to her.*

Angel gives an appreciative smile but shakes her head. She looks down at Princess and says, "You know?" Angel asks, expectantly, "When Jerome was talking this afternoon?" She stops, gathers her thoughts and says, "I think I know what he meant." Angel smiles. "I think, you're a Mystical Gypsy!" *

Princess looks surprised. "You know, Angel," Princess replies with excited eyes, "You are not the first one to guess that. In the hospital there was a girl named I-yo, well her real name was Iolanda,... but her family was from Romania. And get this." Princess looks at Faith as she continues, "Her mother was from Transylvania,... no really." *

Angel lets out a slight uncomfortable laugh. *

Princess looks back up at Angel. "Anyway, I-yo told me the same thing. Said she I was a Visionary Gypsy. She could see a Violet-purple – Indigo-blue aura around me. Said I was a Daydreamer, a Seeker and, she said that the reason I was hearing voices and seeing things was because at times, other worlds or dimensions would call out to me and reveal their realm to me." *

"Sounds a lot like Doctor Strange." Gladstone comments without turning around. *

"Strange, huh?" Princess replies, sounding mildly irritated to Gladstone. *

Gladstone jumps up from his chair and stands next to Angel. "No, really." Gladstone replies, looking down at Princess. "Doctor Strange is maybe one of the most powerful sorcerers in the world. He has an ability to tap into other-world entities and astral planes from his mystical energy. Energy drawn in by the power of divine beings. This power helps him to be one with the forces of the universe." *

"Sounds like you're talking about 'the Force' there, Skywalker." Princess replies. *

"I was just saying,..." Gladstone replies nonchalantly as he walks back and sits back down. *

Angel looks down at Princess and whispers, "I think he likes you." *

Princess smiles knowingly back and says, "I sense you want to talk about something else." *

Angel looks surprised. "We'll, I,..." She hesitates before continuing, "I don't even know what I want to talk about." Angel replies. "But I just get the feeling that I need to talk to you." *

"Do you want to go somewhere else and talk about it?" Princess asks. *

"I don't know." Angel replies. "These guys here are like, family but,..." *

Princess stands, looks around and says, "I don't know, doesn't look like,..." *

"Let's go over there," Angel points, "behind Bobby's tent." *

The two no sooner get to the spot Angel was pointing to when Princess says softly, "I don't think they can hear us from here,..." She looks over at the crowd huddled around the fire and says loudly, "Can you?" *

"What?" Gladstone replies, puzzled. "Did you need me?" *

"We'll talk about that later." Princess replies loudly. *

"Oh," Gladstone responds somewhat baffled, "Okay." He turns back around and faces the fire. *

Princess turns to Angel and saying softly, "Does it have anything to do with the note in your pocket?" *

"Note in my pocket?" Angel asks astounded. "How did you know about that?" *

"Nothing quite so mystical." Princess responds calmly. "You put your hand in that small pocket of your skirt at least eight times, and from the shape of your hand when it's in that small pocket, it has to be a piece of paper. And I'm guessing that it has something to do with the, 'Paper Heart Spirit' we visited earlier?" *

"Sherlock Holmes." Angel replies. *

"But, no." Princess responds. "What we talked about earlier is done. I feel like,... like there's something else troubling you. And uh, I'm guessing it has to do with,...." *

"I don't know what it is." Angel replies. "I just feel,... I don't know. Maybe it's us moving around again, maybe it's leaving school here, but no, it's something else." *

"Hmm," Princess says, Would you like to do another, 'Expressive Arts Therapy' thing?" *

"What do you mean?" Angel asks, in disarray. *

"Let's do this." Princess replies. "You stand there and close your eyes," Princess watches as Angel closes her eyes. "Now, think about you being somewhere else, far from here or anywhere you even know about. Yes, that's right, you are somewhere you've always wanted to be." Princess lets a small silence pass and then asks, "Where are we now, Angel?" *

Angel does not answer, but after a moment she is softly humming to the tune, 'trouble' and swaying. *

"Do you know where you are?" Princess asks then quickly questions knowingly, "Are you on a stage?" *

"Yes." Angel replies. "Yes, I'm on a stage." *

"And are you alone?" *

"No,..." Angel answers, "There's others here too,... they're,... they're dressed,... nicer, and,..." Angel sways back and forth as she says, "they move so more graceful than me,..." Angel's face grows suddenly melancholy and gloomy and she asks, "Can I open my eyes now?" *

"If you want to, you can but," Princess reports, "if you want to find out what it is, this thing that's bothering you, well, we need to stay on the stage a little longer. What do you want to do?" *

"I,... I'll stay on the stage." Angel says nervously. *

"This stage you're on," Princess notes, "what are the others there doing?" *

"Dancing." Angel curtly reports. *

"Hmm." Says Princess. "And you're there on the stage with them, dancing?" *

"Yeah." Angel answers. "But,... they're dancing over there and I'm dancing over here." *

"By yourself?" Princess asks. *

"Yeah." Angel answers. *

"Can you move yourself," Princess asks, "or, let's say, dance yourself over to where they are?" *

"I'm trying," Angel says as she sways gently, moving herself over by a foot, "but I can't do it." *

"Hey there." Princess calls out softly. "Let's not worry about you going over there. Are you having fun dancing where you are?" *

"Yeah," Angel calls back questioningly with a soft voice like she is far away, "but I'm,... I'm kind of worried about the other dancers knowing,..." *

"Knowing what?" Princess asks. "What is it that you're afraid they'll know,..." *

"Doesn't matter," Angel says with resignation. "I'm pretty sure they know, they're just being nice about it." *
"What do they know?" Princess asks. *

"They know about me." Angel says as her swaying slows down to a stop. *

"What do they know about you, Angel," Princess asks, "that

makes you feel sad enough to cause you to have to stop dancing? Angel, what do you think is wrong with you?" *

There is a long pause before Angel asks, "Can I open my eyes again?" *

"That depends," Princess answers, "are you hurting too much to go on or do you want to find out how to get past this problem?" Princess waits for an answer but when none comes, she says, "It's up to you, Angel. This is all about you and how you identify and comprehend yourself. I know it's hard to let on, but can you try to tell me what you think the other dancers know?" *

"They know," Angel replies sheepishly, "that I can never be as good as they are." *

"Are they laughing at you or,..." Princess begins. *

"No." Angel interrupts, "they're nice. They're just,..." *

"Angel," Princess says, questioningly, "why are the other dancers better than you? Is it because of where you live and your circumstances as a homeless person?" *

"No." Angel answers. "It's not that." *

"Well then," Princess asks, "Why are the other dancers better than you?" *

There is a pause before Angel answers, "They can glide and move graciously; they don't have to worry about being top heavy." *

"Top heavy?" Princess asks thoughtfully. "So, you're saying that you're top heavy?" *

"Yes." Angel replies. "And everybody knows that women that are top heavy can never become ballet dancers. I mean, successful dancers on the stage." Tears start filling Angel's eyes. *

"I see." Princess replies. "So,..." Princess begins as she steps over to where Angel is standing and she puts her hand on Angel's shoulder. "I'm not sure where to start here." She pauses to think and says, "Well first, you need to keep your eyes closed. Second, you need to pretend like those other dancers have stopped dancing and are all looking over at you. Can you do that?" *

"Yeah." Angel replies reluctantly. "But I don't like them looking at me." *

"Oh, never mind them." Princess says happily. "Now, I want you to listen for the music. Do you hear it? The music is calling for you to dance. Can you hear it? When you can hear the music, start dancing again. Can you do that for me? For you?" *

Angel starts to sway gently to and fro, slowly moving from side to side, then repeatedly flowingly from one place to another and back again. *

"That's good, Angel." Princess declares. "What I want you to realize is that the music you're hearing, that you're dancing to is the music in your heart. It's always been there for you, but sometimes you hear others dancing to their music and you think you need to dancing to their music instead. Their music is more accepted out there in the world and you want your dancing to be validated too, right?" *

Angel's dancing takes a slight jerking motion but she rights herself. *

"Your dance, Angel," Princess reports, "is nothing like anyone else's dance in the world. Pretend that the other dancers are now dancing on the side of you. Can you see that even if they try to dance with your heart-felt music, that can't. They're used to following the rules and regulations and timings that they were taught to, to do their dance. But you, Angel. You don't have to follow any rules. You are free. Free to dance the way you will, top heavy by their standards, but perfect by yours." *

Angel starts to pick up her pace, moving from side to side with confidence, then continually streaming gracefully, circling from one place to another and back again. *

"That's it." Princess exclaims. "You are the best at what you do when you stop comparing yourself with others and instead dance with the tenderness and passionate love that you have in your heart." *

As Angel dances joyfully around, she asks, "Can I open my eyes now?" *

"If you wish to," Princess says, "but there's still one more thing we might want to attend to here, right?" *

"Oh," Angel replies with a note of curiosity as she spins around, "What is that?" *

"Angel," Princess asks, "What are the other dancers doing right now?" *

"They're,..." Angel begins, "they're gone. Where did they go?" *

"They're still around," Princess replies, "they're just not on the same stage as you anymore. Some of them went to their very own stages, and a few of them gave up after trying to meet the standards of the others." Princess takes a few steps back and says, "Okay, Angel,... one last thing." *

"Okay," Angel says willingly, "what do you want me to do?" *

"We've been so busy with understanding your dilemma," Princess replies, "We never asked why. Why did you feel you weren't good enough? Why did you need to be a good dancer in the first place?" *

"I don't know." Angel answers puzzled, still dancing in small circles. *

"Angel," Princess says gently. "Look out from the stage. Look out into the audience. Let the lights to the theatre be partially dimmed so you can look out into the faces of your audience and,... can you see the faces of the people looking back at you?" *

Angel stops dancing and with eyes still closed, she peers out into the darkness and replies, "well,..." *

"Yes?" Princess questions, "Who do you see?" *

"Tears again roll out of Angel's closed eyes and down her cheek as she answers, "My mother." She sobs for a moment and says, "the only one in the audience is my mother." *

"And do you know why the only one in the audience is your mother?" Princess asks. *

"Duh." Angel answers, wiping way her tears with the sleeve of her long-sleeve tee shirt. "Because she's my mom. Because she's the one that's always there for me. She's the one that I have to take care of because she doesn't take care of herself. Because she's the one that loves me maybe as much as I love her." *

"Class dismissed." Princess says smiling. "You can now open your eyes and Angel, please don't suppress or stifle you good heart and sincere wonderfulness. You are a special 'one of a kind' spirit, and know that the world is blessed with you being; with you bringing out your brilliant art and just being here for us to revile in and to share. The world is already suffering far too much from the lack of genuine, unpretentious goodness and originality. It needs; we need, that luminosity that people like you bring to it." *

With eyes now open and with a contented smile on her face, Angel lightly dances away. *

From the opposite direction Princess spies Scrounge stepping seemingly out of nowhere to go to sit by the fire, and though their eyes never meet, from the look on Scrounges' face, Princess knows that Scrounge was there and that she knows. *

As Princess goes and sits down next to Faith, Faith says, "Thank you for doing that. I been trying to tell her that for weeks." *

"I bet you have, Faith." Princess replies. *

"You know," Hoot says, looking down at Princess but talking loud enough for anyone to hear and hoping Gladstone is paying attention, "I think it's providence that brought you here and into our lives." Hoot smiles wryly as he says, "Faith and I here are thinking about moving back to "the Jungle" and,..." *

"Hoot, you just stop it right now." Faith interjects with a tone of anger in her voice. "You know darn well we'd rather go just about anywhere before we went back there. Anyway, we're heading over to space 28 in the new mitigation site tomorrow and she knows it." *

Hoot chuckles. "I was just,..." *

"You were just shaking the tree to see if an apple might fall." Faith interrupts again. Faith turns to Princess and says, "But don't you worry, we'll make sure you're taken care of." *

"Well, as I was saying," Hoot says as he turns to the fire to warm himself, "I think it was providence that brought you here to be with us, Princess." Hoot looks at Faith who contorts a smile back at him. "Yeah," Hoot says as he positions himself to warm his hands next to Gladstone, "The universe works in mysterious ways." He leans over a bit and says, "Jerome, have you ever had one of those strange; 'this is the universe trying to tell me something' moments?" *

"Yeah," Jerome answers, "and I try to get an enmity between myself and that moment." *

"Enmity." Faith replies. "That's a good biblical word." *

"Yeah," Jerome replies, "Enmity, which is derived from an Anglo-French word meaning "enemy" suggesting either an overt or a concealed hatred." *

"Really?" Faith questions. "I didn't know that." *

"How about you, Gladstone?" Hoot says, looking over to him. "Have you ever experienced one of those, 'universe' moments?" *

Hoot is surprised to see the look of confusion on Gladstone's face as he gets out of the camping chair and steps over to where Faith and Princess are sitting. *

"Yes." Gladstone answers, looking directly into Princess's eyes with an awkward look on his face. "Yes, I have." He says as he reaches down with his hand and gently lifts Princess up to a standing position, all the while looking in her eyes. *

Gladstone stands by his tent with a hand touching the top as he reaches into a coat pocket and pulls out a harmonica and plays an interlude to the song, then he smiles at Princess, and embarrassingly says, "Huh," Before he quickly regains his courage and sings to Princess; **'I'll Make A Space For You'**

43

I'll Make A Space For You

Huh, I'll make a space for you
to step into my life;
as I open up my heart
to be with you here tonight.
And I know we need to be honest
with each other to get by,
so, I'll make a space for you
that you might step here in my life.
Mm, step here in my life.
Well, I'll make a space for you
that we might further the cause;
that recognizes magnetism
without hesitation or pause,
and I know you know about trouble
that can haunt us day and night,
but I'll make a space for you,
should you want to be in my life.

Mm, yeah, to be in my life.

I'll make a space for you
where you can feel at ease
to maybe find yourself in love
and go as fast, or slow as you please.
And I know that it's never easy
to finally get up the courage and try,
still, I'll make a space for you,
in hopes you might step into my life.
You might step into my life.
And I know you're deeply aware
of what can happen over time,
so, I'll make a space for you, Babe
For when you're ready to step into my life.
Mm, ready to step into my life.

As Gladstone finishes his song, he throws his harmonica to Hoot who plays the harmonica to the ending music. Meanwhile Gladstone takes a willing and happy Princess in his arms and together they happily dance a kind of lilting country loop-around square dance till the music ends

44

ACT TWO - SCENE SIX

ACT TWO — SCENE SIX:

The Players:
**HOOT, GLADSTONE, JEROME, PRIVATE,
PRINCESS, FAITH, BOBBY, SCROUNGE & ANGEL**

THE TENT CIRCLE: It's maybe two in the morning. Scrounge and Angel's voices can be softly heard from their flashlight-lit up tent. Bobby is standing just outside her tent. Princess is in Hoot and Faith's tent with Faith. Hoot, Gladstone, Jerome and Private are sitting in camping chairs, huddled around the 10,000 BTU portable propane heater and discussing their circumstances. *

"I think I may be heading to the 4th Ave bridge tomorrow,... uh, I mean, today." Private reports. *

"Mos Eisley Spaceport." Gladstone reports, looking into the glow of the propane heater. *

Hoot replies. "You will never find a more wretched hive of scum and villainy." *

"I know, I know." Private replies, "Already met Jimbo; the boss. But he actually keeps a tight ship, man, that's for certain." Private grins and continues, "I already a got come-ahead from him to go there. He's like, ex-marine. And, I think he's keen on vets." *

"Be mindful of your thoughts," Gladstone replies, "they betray you." *

Private looks confused as he says, "Least that's what he led me to believe. He likes Dumpster here, too." Private continues with less confidence in his conversation. "I kind a believe that he'd like to Shanghai him and make him a venomous guard dog. That ain't happening." *

"Good thing too." Gladstone replies. "Hs's a good dog. But he needs somebody besides that scurvo. Dumpster needs someone that has,... I don't know, a woman's touch?" *

"Okay, okay." Private surrenders. "I was supposed to go sleep there, but I am having second thoughts. But after my friends in, 'the Circle' get scattered to the four winds, not sure where I'll go." *

"I feel embarrassed," Hoot says, "that I haven't take action before this. Seems I'm always waiting to the last minute with a hope and a prayer, wishing something will come up at the last minute to keep us all together. But all the rules have changed. I'm working to get back to normalcy." *

"Kind of like the rest of us." Jerome replies. *

Hoot tries to turn up the valve to the heater only to find it's already turned up all the way. "I've always been behind the curb." Hoot says regretfully. "When I was a younger man, (a much younger man), I had this thing,… this need to create in my heart; in the very fiber of my being and from the time I was fourteen, I knew I was supposed to be a singer, songwriter, musician, performer." *

"And a good one you are." Gladstone reports. *

Hoot looks over with a slight smile and replies, "It's been a long road. Come a long way." *

"I'm gonna do the same thing." Gladstone replies smiling brightly. *

"I'd be lying to you," Hoot says, less happy, "if I told you it'll be a good way to go. It's a long, hard road that, if you're seeking fame and fortune or even validation, leads to disappointment and heartache." *

"But you're great, man" Jerome replies. "Why would you say that,…" *

"I thought I was good back then, I was always pretty good," Hoot replies, "but I was always behind the curve. All the time, I felt it was my destiny. I'd work all day to feed the family and pay the bills, but in truth, I was never very successful in my various jobs; still, we got by." *

"Seen a lot a hard times." Private interjects. "Another man might a given up. You didn't." *

"Yeah, but like I said, it was my destiny to do this songwriting thing, so after everyone was asleep in bed, I'd stay up late into the night and write lyrics;" Hoot turns to Gladstone and continues, "creating new works of art, (or so I thought them to be) and then, I'd take those lyrics that I'd written the night before, and I would refine the stanzas, sharpen the meaning to the words and come close to perfecting the expressions, and then, I'd create musical backgrounds to accompany the words; to have the words and music come together in a kind of marriage." *

"Sweet." Gladstone replies. *

Hoot smiles and says, "It was sweet. Even sweeter when I'd play the songs with my Guitar, over and over and over until I was sure that that song would be polished or at least what I hoped had the magic, and then I'd keep playing that song over and over again until I committed it to my memory." *

"That must a been kind a hard," Private remarks, "keeping up your ambitions while knowing that your audience was so limited." *

"Yeah," Hoot responds, "but it was the promise of the future that drove me on. And that process went on like that all through the seventies and the eighties." *

"That's a lot of stuff to have to commit to memory." Jerome adds. "All the words and the music." *

"It was." Hoot admits. "But when I worked at the funeral home I,…" *

"You worked at a funeral home?" Private asks. *

"For about three years." Hoot replies. "But that gave me time to type up the words to my songs and it gave me a chance to create new songs." Hoot laughs. "I even had an old beater guitar stashed in the Cherrywood casket in the back room. And when business was dead,…" *

"Business was dead?" Jerome parrots incredulously and laughs. *

"Sorry," Hoot replies, "Thought I wore that one out a long time ago." Hoot laughs and continues. "So, I got me this 4-track cassette recording unit? And I started recording my songs, first with just guitars and harmonicas, and I recorded, what I thought was my best material, and I created four albums with about 45 minutes on each of em. That was so I could put two albums on a single 90-minute cassette." *

"Wow." Gladstone replies, "that must a been great. Do you still got em?" *

"Sure." Hoot replies. "And they've kind of stood up over time." Hoot looks off reflectively and continues. "Yeah, but you know? I always wanted to see what my music would sound like electrified, you know, with a bass and percussion and electric guitars and stuff,…?" *

"So, you got together in a band?" Jerome asks. *

"No,... well, yeah, I did get into a band for a while; they were in Tenino, long drive there and back for rehearsals, twice a week, but they only liked me for my harmonica and they only wanted to do covers." *

"So you quit?" Jerome asks. *

Yeah," Hoot answers, "You're in bars doing country western, but the worse thing is; I don't like doing covers. You're always being compared to how well you play John Fogerty's Proud Mary, or George Strait's Amarillo By Morning. If I do me, well I can only be compared to me." *

"Makes sense." Private replies. *

"And doing me got better," Hoot replies, "when I was able to create a wall of sound after I borrowed Cousin Martha's old Casio keyboard for about three or four months. You might remember those keyboards in the eighties? Had like, these funky midi sounds and cartoonish percussion patterns? Well anyway, I decided to in-corporate those groovy sounds and far-out drum patterns, working em in with my material and with what guitars and harmonicas I had, and I created another four and a half albums with the Casio keyboard." *

"That's a lot of songs, right?" Jerome asks. *

"Yeah," Hoot answers, "and I thought I was something. And I'm making demo tapes and sending em to record companies; oh, my gosh, so many record companies; Columbia, Elektra, Warner Broth-ers, RCA, Apple, Atlantic, Capitol, Epic, Decca, Polydor, MCA, and I got responses back from some of em, telling me my stuff was too personal, keep working on it, you'll get it someday; I saved all the reject letters, mostly in hopes to say to them later when I made it, hey, look what you lost out on." Hoot checks the valve again. "Faith threw em all away one day when I wasn't looking. Didn't want me dwelling on the negativity of it all." *

"But four and a half?" Gladstone parrots. "Why four and a half?" *

"Cousin Martha wanted her keyboard back." Hoot replies grinning. "But it was good while it lasted" *

"What'd you do to fill up the other half an album?" Gladstone asks. "Or did you?" *

"Oh yeah," Hoot answers. "I was gifted another keyboard. This new keyboard was hot off the presses for the year 1992; a Yamaha, model PRS-500." *

"That sounds awesome." Jerome replies excitedly. "So then what'd you do?" *

"I picked up where I left off, and again, after everyone was asleep, I'd record one song after another; all of them songs I'd written along the way; all the songs I'd spent the last 25 years creating. And another really cool thing happened; more songs were coming out and I mixed them with my older material and kept recording albums; another 35 albums to be exact." *

"Another 35 albums?" Gladstone asks amazed. "That's a lot of material." *

"Well," Hoot says looking down, "I did rerecord some of my

material with the newer instruments and, six of the albums were purely instrumental stuff; musical compositions and musical ideas to put words to, at some other time. Which, I did do a couple of times, but I was on a roll and I couldn't take the time to go back when all this new stuff was coming in." *

"That is truly amazing." Private reports. "Astounding." *

"Astounding." Hoot laughs cautiously. "That'd be a word, I think, for Faith." *

"Yeah, maybe." Private muses. "That is truly an accomplishment though. I'm surprised you never got found out. I mean, wow, man. That's like,... 45 albums, right?" *

"Yeah." Hoot replies, looking across the sea of tents. "Truly an accomplishment." Hoot pauses with his thoughts for a moment and says kindly, "Good math, Private." Hoot takes in a deep breath and says unexcitingly, "That was my analog years." Hoot looks up with pursed lips before saying, "In my digital-two-point-oh era, after I got an eight-track-digital recorder and using computer technology, this time I'm recording onto CDs, which now allowed me to put 60 to 80 minutes on the disks,..." Hoot smiles resignedly. "I recorded another 20 albums." *

"Another freaking 20 albums?" Gladstone exclaims. "You're kidding me, man." *

"You're killing me." Jerome roars disbelievingly. "I just don't get it." *

"yeah, well," Hoot says without emotion, "I kept thinking

someone would find me out there on YouTube and tell some friends and they'd tell others,..." Hoot stops, collects his thoughts and says, "But that never happened. That next song to get me noticed? Or that entrepreneur that's been looking for me from afar, that wanted to discover someone like me to take me to the top? Or some well-known, legendary performer, singer, celebrity, whatever,... might contact me at my web page and let me know that they want to do something with my material?" Hoot stands, walks around and sits down again. "Problem is, when I was younger, I was just not good enough." *

"Come on," Jerome questions, "You're great." *

"And now? I'm too old." Hoot says dubiously, "No one wants to take a chance with someone that's gonna die in ten years,... or sooner." Hoot looks up at the sky and all the bright stars in the night and says, "Dreams die hard. You know Gladstone, the animation where there's the angel on the right shoulder and the devil on the left?" *

"Yeah, Gladstone replies. "Classic. Well, there's the Donald Duck cartoon, 1938 "Donald's Better Self," written by Carl Barks by the way, where Donald has the angel Donald and the devil Donald fighting over his daily life choices, and then there's The Emperor's New Groove, 1999, no, 2000 I think, well it's where Kronk is confused whether or not he should do the right thing and he has this tiny angel on his right shoulder and this tiny devil on his left and they're fighting over,..." *

"We get the picture." Jerome says, annoyed. *

"Well," Hoot expounds, "on my right shoulder, 'the angel,' I think, is telling me that I gotta keep chasing that dream, you know? And on my left shoulder, 'maybe the devil,' tells me that if I wanna be happy, I'm gonna have to take my head out of the clouds and come to the realization that it ain't never gonna happen." *

But what if the devil and the angel switches messages," Jerome interjects,... *

"You mean," Hoot replies with a sly grin, "what if the devil is telling me I gotta keep chasing that dream and the angel is saying for me to take my head out of the clouds and quit? Don't know." *

"Quite a conundrum." Private replies. "Lot of conflict going on with you, man." *

"Yeah, Hoot replies knowingly, "Lot of conflict going on." Hoot reaches into a coat pocket and pulls out his, 'A' harmonica and plays an interlude to the song before singing, **'Fading Away'**

45

Fading Away

I had me this dream years ago; it was such a sweet dream,
and I was working hard to make it all mine
I thought I knew what to do; how to get what I wanted;
it'd all just be a matter of time.
Something went wrong along the way, I lost focus
along with everything else, with a really bad hand
and I,.. I had a plan B and an ace up my sleeve
but things didn't play out as planned.
Now I'm sitting here, staring into space,
thinking of how life is fickle
As some, might have beens march by like a parade,
yeah, yeah,.. and the lights from the dream of mine
are still bright as day
but me, I'm fading away; I'm fading away.

It was another bad year again for me,
and you know the future ain't looking so bright,

as options keep falling away; I get behind,
but hey man, I'm still in the fight.
There's a cold wind's blowing these autumn days,
it's hard to feel motivated and it's even harder to try.
Though all the rules have changed I'm working to get back
to my inspirations that haven't run dry.
Being here in this place is kind a bizarre,
but when you're down and out
You can't be choosy where you stay
no, no, so I'm huddled by this fire working on a new idea
but unlike my ambition, I'm fading away; Uh, fading away.

I walk the streets at night unnoticed like a ghost
planning how to jumpstart my life's next move
And I'm pushing back all of the negative forces
cause I can feel I got something to prove;
Yeah

As each new day comes and goes, I wonder
if things for me will ever shift into another gear
I gotta rise from adversity or else
I'm doomed to live the rest of my life here.
And I'm out here with the ranks of the irrelevant
With the poor, the forgotten, the lost,
and like them, I've become mostly invisible, unwanted
especially after all the lines that I've crossed.
My importance, my relevance, my value
is in the eye of the beholder to weigh
Yeah, I'm still working that dream as my time will allow
I feel I'm getting closer,
but, I'm fading away; huh, fading away.

46

ACT TWO - SCENE SEVEN

DEEP INSIDE THE TENT CAMP: "Who is this woman, Alanna?" Jerome asks as he and Private walk towards the back portion of the tent encampment. "Do I know her?" *

"I don't know." Private answers with Dumpster happily walking along. "Do you?" *

"I don't know." Jerome answers. "Who's on first?" *

"That's right." Private answers. "Who's on first, What's on second, and I Don't Know's on third."

"That's what I want to find out." Jerome says. *

"I say," Private answers. "Who's on first, What's on second, I Don't Know's on third." *

"I'm confused," "Jerome reports, "So tell me, who's on first?" *

Private answers, "Yes." *

"I mean the fellow's name." Jerome presses. *

Private answers, "Who." *

"The guy on first." Jerome clarifies. *

Private answers, "Who." *

A little irritated, Jerome says, "The first baseman." *

Private answers, "Who." *

"The guy playing..." Jerome begins. *

Private answers, but with a note of annoyance, "Who is on first!" *

Jerome replies with a louder voice of annoyance, "I'm asking YOU who's on first." *

"That's the man's name." Private answers. *

Jerome with a louder voice of irritation asks, "That's who's name?" *

Private calmly but distinctly answers, "Yes." *

Jerome replies, "Well go ahead and tell me." *

"That's it." Private replies, mildly angry. *

"That's who?" Jerome asks. *

"Exactly." Private replies and laughs. *

"So we're going over to,…" Jerome questions. *

"We're going over to the old railroad tracks down the street from the far corner of the lot." Private answers. "She said there was a dog there that someone ditched when they left camp earlier today." *

"Ditched?" Jerome asks. *

"That's what Alanna said." Private replies. "And I just want to see if it's still there and if it needs help or food or something." *

As they walk, they go past tent after tent, and see most of the people are not going to sleep or packing their stuff up, but instead, they see most of the tents internally lit up and there are loud conversations going on inside, and, in spite of the fact that it is a very cold night, partying is happening inside and outside of the tents. *

"Aren't you cold?" Jerome asks, looking at Private. *

"Not really." Private answers. "This m65 jacket is warmer than you think." *

"Well I'm freezing." Jerome reports. "I should a put on my other sweater." *

"You got two on already." Private mentions, "And you got like three tee shirts under that." *

"True that." Jerome says, shivering. "Can't be too careful these days." *

"From the look of all the garbage scattered around," Private says stepping over unceremoniously abandoned trash and debris hard to discern in the darkness, "Doesn't look like any of these guys believed in the moratorium." He tugs at Dumpster's leash and says, "Don't eat that junk. You don't know where it came from and it'll make you sick." *

"Did you believe in the moratorium?" Jerome asks as they negotiate their way through narrow unorganized walkways and between disorderly and chaotic tent sites, almost tripping on the piles of garbage. *

"No, not really." Private answers. "But I did see you out there picking up everybody else's rubbish." *

"True that." Jerome replies uncomfortably. "I was uh, just covering all the bases." *

"Hope springs eternal." Private says, agreeably as they come to a spot where the fence is closed. *

"Why is the fence closed?" Jerome asks. "And it looks like the gate is,..." *

With a swift steadying hand on Jerome's shoulder Private stops suddenly and looks around cautiously. "Shh." He quietly responses and gives a perceptive tug on Dumpster's leash to alert him be vigilant but quiet. Private turns his head slightly, listening and whispers, "Something's wrong here." He strains as he scans through the darkness and whispers loudly, "Roger!" *

The word no sooner leaves Private's lips and there is the sound of a gunshot. Private falls to the ground, his hand seems to tug on Jerome's clothing as he goes down. *

"Private!" Jerome calls out as he goes down to search Private's body to see what his condition is. *

Meanwhile, after the gunshot rings out, Dumpster no sooner shoots out into the darkness toward the source of the gunshot, when there is a sound of him suddenly running out of tether. Jerome imagines that the handle of Dumpster's leash may be caught on some unknown object or piece of garbage. As Dumpster is abruptly stopped somewhere in the darkness, Dumpster is verbally silent, but Jerome can faintly hear the sounds of something struggling; like the sounds of a dog's legs scratching to brake free. *

Another shot is fired. Jerome instinctively lies down on the ground next to Private's lifeless body, but Jerome quickly realizes that he is still a target. He half stands, turns and runs, helter-skelter, as fast as he can, falling over debris, getting back up, falling again, getting up and zigzagging his way through the tent maze till he gets to the sidewalk on State Avenue. *

Feeling himself vulnerable and exposed, and likely still a target for Roger, he stands only a moment under the streetlights before he sprints in front of oncoming cars, across State Street, and with his heart pounding in his head, he races two blocks down on Adams Street sidewalks before turning down Fifth Avenue and stops. Finding himself in front of the Rainy-Day Records shop, he gasps for air as he looks desperately around in all directions. *

After he catches his breath, Jerome takes off running again with no care in what direction as long as it is away from where he was. Turning up Franklin Street, he can hear the sound of sirens in the distance. Moments later, Jerome ironically finds his way back to, 'the Circle' where all of his friends are huddled together talking excitedly to each other. *

47

ACT TWO - SCENE
EIGHT

The Players:
JEROME, HOOT, BOBBY, FAITH,
GLADSTONE, PRINCESS & SCROUNGE

EXT. THE TENT CIRCLE: When Jerome steps forward, he is surrounded by his friends that want to tell him the news. *

"There's been a shooting." Hoot declares with a look of anxiety and apprehension. *

"Yeah," Bobby interjects. "Police got him though." She smiles uneasily and says, "Turns out it was Roger and some of his friends. I always kind a felt it was gonna end up like this with him" She looks around and asks, "Where's Private?" *

"Yeah, where's Private?" Faith asks, troubled. "Wasn't he with you?" *

"Private was the one that got shot." Jerome reports, apprehensively. *

"What?" Bobby questions disbelievingly looking in Jerome's tear-filled eyes. "Are you sure?" *

"Private and I,... we were going,... I don't even know who we were going to help, but then,..." Shock fills Jerome's face as he stops talking and tries to form the right words. "There was, there was a shot and Private fell to the ground." Jerome looks away before saying, "How could we have been so stupid? We just walked into an ambush set up by Alanna." *

"Alanna," Questions Hoot. "Are you sure?" Hoot looks to Faith. "She must have been promised something special to betray her friend, Private like that." *

Faith nods and says, "Best not judge until you know all the facts,..." *

"Even Judas had his price." Bobby replies with a strong note of anger. *

"After I heard the second gunfire,..." Jerome looks down, ashamed. "Private was just lying there,... and I,... I got scared. I,... I just got up and ran away." Jerome breaks down. *

"That was the right thing to do." Faith says gently, touching Jerome's shoulder to comfort him. *

Jerome quickly pulls himself away and says, "But I left him there on the ground. I just ran away." *

"And what good would it have done you," Gladstone remarks, "if you'd stayed there? You fell into an ambush and,... and what if you were Roger's target all along? He hated you more than Private. What if that second shot was meant for you, Jerome? And if you hadn't run a third or fourth bullet might have gone and killed you!" *

"Gladstone is right." Princess remarks. "Jerome, you did the right thing." *

"What happened to the Dumpster?" Bobby asks, looking around like he should be there amongst them. *

"I don't know." Jerome answers. "It was dark and we couldn't see very well, and when Private fell, Dumpster took off towards where the shot was fired, and then I heard him squeal like he had hit something or,... I don't know; but when the second shot was fired, I didn't hear him anymore. I didn't hear anything anymore. I don't know; I just ran away." Jerome sits on the curb with his head in his hands. *

"I'm gonna go over there and find out what's happening to Private." Says Hoot. *

"Honey," Faith says worriedly, "I don't know,..." *

"Listen," Hoot replies, "Roger's already been picked up. Any of his other cronies have either gotten picked up too or they've gone into hiding and,... we need to know what's happening with our friend, Private." Hoot gives Faith a quick kiss on the side of her face and asks, "Where's that bright flashlight I got at Harbor Freight?" *

Faith goes into her tent for a second, come back out. "Here." She says, handing Hoot the flashlight. *

Jerome looks up and half-heartedly says, "I'm gonna go with you." *

"No," Hoot says sternly, "You don't want to be associated with any of this or with Roger. I promise I'll find out and let you know." *

Gladstone looks down at Jerome as he puts his hand on Jerome's shoulder. Looking up at Hoot, he says, "I'm going with you." *

"Who's the more foolish?" Hoot asks. "The fool or the fool who follows him?" *

"I'm going." Gladstone replies smiling. *

Hoot soberly nods approvingly and together; Hoot and Gladstone walk away. *

Moments later, Jerome gets up, walking to his tent he sees Hoot's 'Guitar with No Strings' resting in its guitar stand just outside Hoot's tent. Jerome picks it up and walks to one of the camp chairs by the fire, (propane heater) and sits down. *

As the music starts, Jerome starts playing the 'Guitar with No Strings' and then soberly sings, **'Ya Gotta Move On'**

48

❦

Ya Gotta Move On

You find yourself at times
wanting to correct resolve or renew
the broken, the lost, the ended,
when there's nothing you can do.
There's a mindset that you gotta fix or try to right the wrong,
but there comes a time to let go
and ya gotta move on.

*(After Jerome finishes singing the first verse, he picks up and plays a
slight riff on Hoot's 'Guitar with No Strings') ***

After things went sideway what happened?
You're not really sure,
but all you really want is for the things
to get back to the way they were.
But like time, you gotta push forward
with a lesson to build upon,

knowing tomorrow follows today
and ya gotta move on.

*(After Jerome finishes singing the second verse, he again picks up and plays a slight riff on Hoot's 'Guitar with No Strings') ***
You want a grasp over matters that occur
but you can't change things to the way they were.
It's good sense to see the wrong path
before you go too far,
and it's a wise man
that can accept things as they are;
Oh,...

(Jerome plays yet another small riff on the 'Guitar with No Strings' just before he gets a sad, far-away look in his eyes as he's looking above the audience and gently begins the last verse)

Seems like they're in the next room
just waiting for you to come out,
and you had so much left to tell them
what can you do or say now?
It seems like they were just here
but now, they're finished and they're gone,
and now it's your time to let em go;
ya gotta move on,...
Ya gotta move on.

After finishing singing the ending verse, *Jerome picks up and plays riffs on the, 'Guitar with No Strings' to the end of the song before he slumps down and sits on the pavement looking down at his shoes, lost in sad defeat.*

49

ACT TWO - SCENE NINE

ACT TWO — SCENE NINE:

The Players:
FAITH, PRINCESS, GLADSTONE, JEROME,
HOOT, BOBBY, & SCROUNGE

EXT. THE TENT CIRCLE: As Hoot and Gladstone enter back into, 'the Circle,' Hoot looks back at Faith with a sober knowing glance and as everybody in, 'the Circle' gathers around, Hoot says, "There was a small place cordoned off,... a lot of police. They pretty much told us all to go back to our places and keep packing." *

"What about Private?" Bobby asks, looking quickly over at Jerome who is looking back at Hoot. "Did you guys find,..." *

"I talked with a girl that said she was there." Gladstone answers. "Right after she heard the shooting; she saw police run in and apprehend Roger and one other guy." Gladstone looks over at Jerome.

"There wasn't any sign of Private or Dumpster." Gladstone turns to Bobby as he continues, "I went up to one of the policemen there; a kind of a rude fellow, and asked if anyone was shot when Roger fired his gun. He told me that the incident was still an ongoing investigation and that he, (of course), couldn't comment on anything at that time." *

"What does that mean?" Jerome asked angrily. "They're withholding information about Private?" Jerome scoffs. "Probably gonna keep it all hidden due to the incompetence of our beloved law enforcement." *

"I think," Hoot replies, "that the police were doing everything the way they should have been, to maintain safety. They all looked to be genuinely concerned for everybody's welfare." *

"Sorry." Jerome replies, "Force of habit." Jerome looks to everybody's faces and asks, "But I'd still like to know what happened to Private,..." *

"That girl I was talking to?" Gladstone interjects, "She said that there wasn't any emergency vehicle coming or going. If they'd found someone with a gunshot wound, alive or dead, they would have had to transport him to the hospital. Standard procedures, man." *

"Well, I'm confused." Bobby reports. "What happened to Private?" *

"Hey," Princess says as she stands next to Faith who is sitting on a blanket outside her tent, typing into her laptop. "I wanted to thank you for being so good to me." *

"Oh, sweetie," Faith says, looking up for a moment with sincere caring eyes, "it's all good. Us fellow travelers need to help each other out when we can; we all need to help each other to get by." *

"I've only been here, I don't know, maybe less than 24 hours," Princess reports, "but I kind of feel like,..." Princess searches for the right words. "I kind a feel like you're kind of like,... my mom, you know what I mean?" *

"That's so nice of you to say." Faith replies tenderly. "But you do remind me of one of my daughters right after she started college up in Bellingham." Faith smiles as she says, "She was so precocious." *

"Precocious," Princess declares, "That sounds like a fifty-cent word." *

"Indeed." Faith replies, laughingly. She looks up at Princess in earnest before returning her attention to her work on her laptop. "I see a lot of young kids come in here after they've been kicked around some," Faith utters softly without looking up from her computer screen, "either by bureaucracy or by bad things that happen in their lives." She looks up into Princess's face and continues, "I can't help but try to do what I can to help them; to steer them in the right direction, to get them out of here and on their way to a better life." *

"Maybe that's what I need to do." Princess asserts. *

Faith sets her computer aside and says, "Would you like to talk a little bit about things? If I am nothing else, I'm a good listener." Faith smiles, "Maybe you could tell me what brought you here." *

"Well," Princess replies smiling brightly, "Gladstone brought me here." *

"Yes," Faith says confirmingly, "but tell me, if it's not too personal, why you're not with your family." *

"Family?" Princess parrots as she sits down next to Faith. "well, you already know I'm crazy and I can be churlish,..." *

"Crazy? I wouldn't say,..." Faith begins with sincere empathy, "and churlish? Really good word, by the way,..." *

"No, no," Princess interrupts, "It's okay. I can easily be ill-natured and I been in and out of a few institutions; I know real crazy from messed up crazy." Princess smiles sadly. *

"You're kind a tough on yourself,..." Faith says with a sad look in her eyes. *

"I know what I am and what I am not." Princess continues. "I did not do well in school. Got kicked out a lot. After I was diagnosed with having the crazy; schizophrenia was the main diagnosis I believe, but hardly conclusive because according to the DSM-5, a diagnosis of schizophrenia needs to,..." *

"DSM-5?" Faith asks. *

"DSM-5 stands for the uh,.. the Diagnostic and Statistical Manual of Mental Disorders,..." Princess expounds nonchalantly. "Uh, Fifth Edition, I believe is the reason for the 5." *

"Oh." Faith replies mildly astonished. *

"Anyway, as I was saying," Princess continues, "a diagnosis of schizophrenia is made if a person has two or more core symptoms; one of which must be hallucinations, delusions, and I been having that going on for years,... but disorganized speech for at least one month? "Uh, disorganized speech, not so much." *

"You seem well acquainted with your ability to speak." Faith agrees. *

"The other core symptoms," Princess continues, "are gross disorganization and diminished emotional expression, both of which I have no correlation to,... Princess stares away as she says, "Anyway, after I was diagnosed with having the crazy it was too much for my father and shortly after, he packed up and left; to which my mother didn't take very well." *

"So sorry, Princess." Faith says softly as she reaches over and puts one of Princess's hands in hers. "Sometimes things go,... sideways but that doesn't mean it's your fault." *

Moved by Faith's kindness, Princess looks down, trying to avoid crying. She finally looks up at Faith with tears and says, "My mother blames me for everything that happened,..." *

"No," Faith counters, "I'm sure she doesn't blame you. She loves you. And,..." *

"No." Princess interrupts. "She may love me but not in the way you do. She loves me obligatorily,.." *

"Obligatorily." Faith interjects, "Impressive word." *

"Thanks." Princess muses. "Anyway, my mother loves me as a matter of imposed moral or legal obligation; nothing else. More than once I've heard her when she talks to the doctors or to my brothers,... like a third person or like I'm not right there in the room with her,... She doesn't pretend,..." *

"I'm sure she,..." Faith begins. *

Princess looks Faith in the eyes and says, "I pretty sure she thinks that I'm so far gone mentally that I don't,... that I couldn't possibly understand what she's saying or what's happening to me." Princess looks off into the darkness as she says, "Fact is, my mother was never happier than the day when I was finally committed to the nut house. I was finally out of her house and she no longer had the imminent responsibility of dealing with me and all my ongoing troubles." *

Faith listens attentively and finally asks, "What are you hoping to do now?" *

"I don't know." Princess answers. "Maybe go back to my car and let them,..." *

"No." Faith interrupts with incredulousness. "Are you messing with me? You know that that's not a good option,... That's just giving in to your desperation. Something I know you don't normally do,... You're stronger than that and you know it,... and anyways,... that path leads to your certain destruction. And I think you know that too. You need to find a new path that will bring you to a place of healing, new beginnings and,..." Faith looks over with compassion and understanding, "maybe forgiveness?" *

"Maybe you're right." Princess says doubtfully. "But I'm confused. Are you telling me I need to forgive or be the one to be forgiven? *

Faith looks up with thoughtfulness in her face but says nothing. *

"Shouldn't my mother be the one to forgive me?" Princess asks. "I didn't treat her badly. I can't help it that my father left her and us. Shouldn't I be the one to be forgiven?" *

Faith looks down in thought before looking back at Princess and answering, "Being trespassed upon is a hard thing to endure, but sometimes it's like an illness that never leaves you. That little thought,... that feeling of being treated harshly over time can grow into something more insipid, like, hatred." *

"First," Princess says calmly, "insipid? Seventy-five-cent word if a penny. And second,..." Princess responds heatedly, "I don't hate my mom.". *

"Of course you don't." Faith replies softly. "But the act? That thing that was done? That is something that you continue to carry inside you. And every time you revisit that thing in your mind or in your heart?" Faith scratches her chin before saying, "You feel the wrong and the injustice; the unfairness of it all; the disappointment; the loss. But that thing or combination of things that you're experiencing feeds into your mind and heart, and over time it grows from a slight irritation or annoyance to a resentment of your being mistreated, till eventually anger takes over as it calls out for a justice that may never happen." *

"So it's okay for her to,..." Princess begins. *

"It was never okay," Faith expounds, "for your mother to take out her apparent marital problems or inability to deal with conflict on you, Princess." Faith searches for the right words and says, "But that thing that is you; your spirit inside; you must feel in your heart that it wants closure. It wants you to move on and heal from the wounds that were inflicted over all those years. It's not that it doesn't care about who hurt you or what was done or why it was unfair, your spirit just wants to be healed." *

"It does?" *

"Oh yes." Faith answers. "And I think deep inside, you feel what I'm talking about. And I gotta say, you may wait a lifetime and never have your mother apologize for the way she treated you, but if you're ever to find peace in your being, you need to forgive her and let it go; your Gypsy inner self needs that." *

"I guess you may be right." Princess confesses sheepishly. *

"And one more thing, Princess;" Faith adds, "And I'm speaking from years of experience. It may not end well. She may not forgive you. She may turn on you, maybe cast all of her frustrations back in your direction. It's not for you to expect that you'll arrive to some compromise or reconciliation, or even her forgiveness; only that you were strong enough and brave enough to reach out and forgive her." *

"When you put it that way," Princess replies, "well, there's a lot to think about." *

"I think you're scaring her." Hoot interrupts. "Just tell her that inside her is an energy field created by intelligent design that surrounds us and penetrates us; it binds the galaxy together." *

"You always have had a way about you with words, Hoot." Faith says, smiling. *

"Thank you dear." Hoot says, sitting down again. "So who you working on right now?" *

"My grandmother's grandmother and her family." Faith answers looking to the screen of her laptop. *

"Really?" Princess asks. "This all sounds problematical." *

"problematical?" Faith parrots. "That's a fairly good word." She laughs before continuing. "It hasn't been too easy because these relatives go back to the southeastern part of Italy in the eighteen-fifties. Luckily the townspeople and churches and government facilities kept records and did their own census recordings in their providences; a place to go where I can gather information. It's kind of like, little puzzle pieces that I gather from reports and archives of marriage registers, death reports, and sometimes there's even accounts that chronicles personal or family histories. And then you connect the puzzle with as many pieces as you can so they can fit together and form a story." *

"When you put it like that," Princess replies, "it sounds really cool. But it seems like, I don't know, maybe a whole lot of detective work for you to have to do to find your family." *

"Funny you use that word," Faith says, smiling. "It's one of those words Hoot uses when he's looking over my shoulder to see what I'm doing." Faith returns her attention back to her laptop and continues, "Also, there's some other person or persons that have done a lot of the indexing for me; translating information from different languages, in this case, mostly names from Italian to English." *

"Did those other people do their own work too?" Hoot asks. *

"You know, that's what's strange." Faith answers as Princess leans over to look into the laptop screen. "It's like someone made this information available but didn't finish the job." *

"Maybe that somebody wanted to be sure that you would put it all together so you should get the privilege to do the temple work yourself." Hoot says, smiling. *

"Temple work?" Princess asks. *

"This thing I'm doing is called genealogy." Faith answers as she stops typing and looks up. "In my case it's kind of like the story of me and how things lead up to me, and my existence, through a study of my ancestors' lives, through the existing records of our families that I try to find, somewhere out there in the world. And we submit these names of distant relatives that we've found and the data associated with those names to our church's database and then we, or some other person, can go to the temple and get their work done." *

"So you connect yourself with your relatives, and,... go to your temple?" Princess questions. "You mentioned temples. Are you folks Jewish? And what do you mean, work done?" *

Faith looks knowingly at Hoot for a second before turning to Princess and answers, "The Hebrew people are not the only faith that has temples. Our church has temples all over the world." *

"But why,..." Princess begins. *

"I think," Hoot interrupts, "you're gonna confuse the heck out of this girl,.. or get her baptized." *

"Hoot," Faith replies, "let me do this." Faith turns and looks Princess in the face before saying, "Princess, temples are a House of the Lord. And not only a House of the Lord, but temples are also where members of the church make and renew our covenants with God; and we perform sacred ordinances such as baptism for the dead, washing and anointing (known as "initiatory"), the endowment, and eternal marriage sealings." *

"Really." Princess replies with a note of confusion. "So, it's a holy place, and,...?" *

"I told you." Hoot replies. "Too much information." *

"No, Hoot." Princess says, "I kind of get it. Like Solomon's Temple, right?" Princess smiles shyly as she says, "Being locked up for all that time gave me a lot of time to read books, including the bible." *

"Yes." Faith answers, looking defiantly at Hoot before turning to Princess. "Just like Solomon's Temple. And we act as stand-ins in the temple to get our ancestors baptized, confirmed and we help them to get their endowments done." *

"Endowments?" Princess asks, looking confused.

Faith smiles. "In the temple we learn of sacred things needed to be exalted into the celestial kingdom." *

"Sounds complicated,..." Princess says with a note of unsureness. *

"Can be a little confusing at first,..." Faith replies, smiling, "but it's simple enough after a while,..." Faith touches Princess's hand. "The real neat thing," Faith continues, her eyes twinkling, "is that I get help all the time,... I go to a computer site, like this one here called, Ancestry; the same site I go to all the time, you know,... just doing my thing? and then, suddenly, I find there's all this new information and stuff; it's like those people that passed away a long time ago are knocking at my door from the other side of the veil,... They've been waiting all that time for me to come along, and they throw out these little bits of knowledge for me to use; little pieces of a puzzle for me to piece together, that, when put together, helps me to connect with others in my family." *

"It must make you happy to know you're helping to gather your family together." Princess replies. *

"It's very fulfilling and even exciting," Faith answers, "when you finally make that connection to someone that has a part of your DNA,... and sometimes there is information in the records that let you know a small part of who they were, like when and where they were married, how many children they had, their struggles, the jobs they had, the conflict they went through in the times they were living." *

"Hearing you tell about it and how much you get out of it,"

Princess replies, "kind a makes me want to get a laptop and do my own uh,..." *

"Genealogy?" Faith interjects. *

"Yeah," Princess answers, "genealogy." *

"By the way," Faith says smiling, "Genealogy is a fairly magnificent word too." Faith returns to her computer, points to some names and says, "My problem is, not enough time to get it all done. You see these names here?" She points to the bottom of the screen. "I'm choosing to leave them for now." *

"Why?" Princess asks. "They're not as valuable?" *

"They're valuable all right." Faith answers. "They're like, the favorites; the easier, predictable names, with straightforward and sure lines; I can come back and work on these,..." She points to the middle of the screen. "But these? A whole lot more work involved. And, time and effort? So much more at stake; older communications; names to be found or maybe lost." *

As music plays Faith looks up at the stars with wonder as she begins to sing; **'Sending Out A Message'**

50

ACT TWO - SCENE TEN

ACT TWO — SCENE TEN:

The Players:
ANGEL, SCROUNGE, PRINCESS, FAITH, BOBBY,
HOOT, GLADSTONE, JEROME & PRIVATE

THE TENT CIRCLE: "Why are you so angry?" Scrounge inquires concernedly to Angel. "Did I do something to upset you?" *

"No." Angel replies curtly, almost heatedly before going back to her packing. *

After seeing Angel's dance abilities and performance and hearing Angel's testimony, all Scrounge wants is to embrace her daughter, but seeing Angel's offhand behavior, Scrounge is convinced that her daughter is having problems and Scrounge backs off. *

Angel grunts loudly when she runs into trouble with the hasp of her luggage. *

Scrounge sits on the floor of the tent and asks, "You wanna talk about it now or later?" *

"I don't wanna talk about it." Angel barks back. "Not now or later." Angel sits down on her cot with her back turned to her mother. *

Scrounge breathes in deeply through her nose, holds her breathe for about five seconds and exhales through her mouth. "I'm sorry." Scrounge declares softly, "I shouldn't have taken things out on you before." She moves over to Angel's cot and sits on the floor next to Angel. "Seems I'm always doing that." Scrounge replies as she gently touches and combs Angel's hair with her fingers.
"This possible move to the new mitigation site has got me nervous and upset." Scrounge says as she stands and takes a step back. "You know that I never liked being held down with rules and regulations. And that new place is rife with em. The city is now gonna be managing and policing the place." *

"They are?" Angel replies. *

"Yeah," Scrounge answers, "and it's not gonna be as free and easy as it is here, and there'll be snitches to report back to the authorities and the camp managers." *

"You don't know that." Angel says suspiciously. *

"Yeah," Scrounge says nodding her head, "I do." Scrounge looks down at the ground as she declares, "When I went over to see where we were on the new list,... I was approached,..." Scrounge looks up seriously at Angel. "Gary over there, said he might be able to fit us in,..." Scrounge smiles wryly and says, "if I'd be a conscientious observer for em." *

"A what?" Angel asks. *

"Conscientious observer." Repeats Scrounge. "That's just another name for an informant; a snitch; a rat." *

"What?" Angel retorts with concern as she looks over at her mother. "Are you gonna do that? What did you tell him?" *

"We didn't get in there yet, did we?" Scrounge answers mildly cross at the insinuation but lightens up and says, "Of course, I said no." Scrounge postures herself diagonally and says, "Well,... I,... I said I'd think about it." *

"That's good." Angel replies, reassured. *

"That's good?" Scrounge replies questioningly. *

"Yes." Angel replies, "It means you didn't sell yourself to get in there." *

Scrounge looks directly at her daughter and exclaims, "Angel, I gotta say, I was really tempted." Scrounge looks away exasperated as she declares, "I got to get you out of this situation somehow or another." *

Angel turns to her mother and says, "So why do we need to go there? Can't we just go with some of these other guys and,..." *

"Go where?" Scrounge answers questioningly. "None of them, except Hoot and Faith, have a plan,... a real plan to relocate themselves." Scrounge looks at Angel and says, "I'm not saying anything bad about any of em. I like em all. And I know that that notice for us to pack up and move, came just six days ago; hardly enough time to get resettled, but, if we get a spot in the new site and,..." *

"And what?" Angel says without looking up. "I really don't want you to be a rat." *

Scrounge smiles to herself about her daughter's integrity. Once again she breathes in deeply through her nose, and exhales through her mouth, purses her lips and looks down while saying, "I made a call to your grandma this afternoon." *

"You did?" Angel asks excitedly, looking up with interest. *

"Yeah," Scrounge answers lethargically, "that's where I was when I was gone for a while this afternoon." *

"Well," Angel asks expectantly, "what'd she say?" *

Scrounge looks away and says, "There was nobody home." *

Angel, looking sad, picks up a pad and a blue colored pencil and starts to draw something. *

"I did leave a message and asked her to call." Scrounge interjects. Seeing Angel's face lighten up again, Scrounge continues. "You don't know what it's like there. It's real hot in the summertime and it's right on the other side of Mount Rainier; They get a lot of snow and it hangs around for months. And you don't know what it's like to live with your grandma and grandpa. There's rules and rules and a lot of rules and,..." *

"But it's gotta be better than this." Angel interrupts, laying down her pad and pencil. "Maybe we could just go there and try it out or something. Worse thing to happen is we see what it's like and then if,..." *

With an anguished look on her face, Scrounge blurts out, emphasizing each painful word, "But my mother. never called me back, sweetie." Scrounge turns away and with a soft, distant voice, she repeats, "She never called me back." *

Angel gets up from her cot, moves to where her mother is standing with her back to Angel. Angel gently puts her hand on one of Scrounges' shoulders and Angel pulls Scrounge around so they're face to face. Angel, with her head slightly bent down, her eyes look up into Scrounges' face, happily says, "Mother, that was the bravest thing I think you have ever done." Angel hugs Scrounge who is seemingly frozen at first but then Scrounge hugs Angel back and Angel rests her head on Scrounges' shoulder. They embrace for a long, silent moment before Angel looks up again into Scrounges' face and replies, "We're gonna be alright, mom. I promise." *

"*You* promise?" Scrounge laughs with a broken voice and forlorn smile. "I'm the one that,... it's my fault that,..." *

Mother." Angel says elatedly as she suddenly breaks the hug and rushes over to her cot. Angel quickly rummages through stuff in a cardboard shoe box and pulls out a pamphlet. "They gave this to me and a couple other kids at school Friday." Angel says, animatedly. "It may be something we could do." *

"What is it?" Scrounge inquires, trying not to look suspiciously at the paperwork her daughter gives her. *

"There was some people that came to visit us, and,..." Angel began. *

Scrounge looks back with a mixture of anger and confusion. "You know me and the state,..." *

"Yeah, yeah." Angel interrupts. "I know we don't have such a good track record with the state, but,..." *

"Not we," Scrounge interrupts, holding the pamphlet like it might be contaminated. "Me, dear. I did it to us." *

"Doesn't matter." Angel says dismissively. "They got a special program for people like us, mother." Angel opens the pamphlet and points with her finger as she reads,

> "If you and your family are experiencing home-lessness or are at risk of becoming homeless, contact us today for more information about how we can help and support your family."

Angel looks at Scrounge hopefully as she continues reading,

> "The Family Support Center is a lead agency

fighting to prevent family homelessness, and is the Coordinated Entry point for all homeless families."

Angel looks in her mother's face and asks, "Doesn't that sound good?" *

Scrounge steps up next to Angel and looks at the paperwork in her hands. *

Angel looks up approvingly and continues reading, *"We work around the clock to ensure no family is left out in the cold."* Angel smiles and says, "That'd be nice, and they provide emergency shelter and housing assistance,..." *

"But, Scrounge contradicts, "what about this?" Scrounge points to a paragraph on the page and skeptically reads out loud, *"Case Management?"* Scrounge looks away as she says, "I told you, I don't want to get involved with the state again. They weren't very nice and,..." Scrounges' voice softens, "I may still owe them money." *

"But," Angel spouts, "It's not a state agency, mother, Look here." Angel points to the paperwork and reads,

> *"The Family Support Center is a nonprofit agency founded in 1992 to provide families and survivors of violence with coordinated, supportive services in one centralized location."* *

"Let me see that." Scrounge says as she gently takes the pamphlet from her daughter's hands. *

As Scrounge holds the paperwork closer, scrutinizing the words, Angel points with her finger as she says, "and they have,... counseling and mental health support," Angel looks up at Scrounge and smiles as she says, "Not that you need mental health support, mom, but it's there if you want it." *

"Thank you dear." Scrounge says playfully. *

Enthusiastically, Angel continues, "and, *life skills*,... don't know what that is. And *advocacy*,... don't know what that is either. But, resources and outdoor living supplies. And computer and phone access! That's pretty neat. Warm clothes and food and hygiene supplies, and transportation? That'd be nice. No more walking up to the westside because we can't afford a bus ticket. And employment assistance." Angel turns to her mother and says, "Maybe they can help you get work." *

Mildly interested, Scrounge reads on and says out loud, "And benefits,..." Scrounge flips the paperwork over one side and back again. "This could be something to look into." Scrounge says positively, "But listen, honey. I don't want you to get your hopes up; it may not happen." *

"I won't." Angel replies, "but there's a 24-hour shelter hotline here too." *

"We'll call tomorrow." Scrounge says smartly. *

Angel goes back to her cot, picks up her pad and pencil and starts drawing again. After a long silence Angel says, "And mom, I wasn't mad at you for taking things out on me." Angel looks over and waits until Scrounge looks back before she continues. "I got this,…" Angel reaches into the tiny pocket of her pink Pastel plaid skirt and pulls out a small ruffled up piece of paper. She waves the piece of paper a few times unceremoniously before putting it back into her skirt pocket. *

"So, what is that?" Scrounge questions, careful not to reveal her knowledge. *

"A note from someone I thought was my friend." Angel replies. "He says in the note that he,…" Angel is silenced as she searches for the words that won't come out. "You know I stayed home from school today,… uh yesterday because of the big move,… uh, today. I'm all messed up." *

"That's okay," Scrounge replies, "So what happened?" *

Angel lifts up her phone and says, "I got a text from my friend, Rose a couple minutes ago." Angel fights tears away as she continues. "Rose sent me a text to let me know that he was walking the halls with Samantha at school today,… yesterday." Angel gulps down the urge to cry but a small whimper escapes. *

"Oh, Angel." Scrounge says sympathetically. She rushes to Angel's rescue, pulls her close into a hugging embrace before exclaiming softly, "I'm so sorry." *

A quiet moment passes before Angel pulls slightly out of the hug to look her mother in the face and then she asks, "What do I do now?" *

Scrounge thinks for a moment before answering, "Move on." *

"That's it?" Angel asks annoyed. "The great words of wisdom; move on?" *

"Angel," Scrounge replies lovingly, "Whatever I say would never be the right thing to say." Scrounge smiles. "Think about it. If I said, "Go to his house and punch him in the face," well that wouldn't do, although you might have thought about it. If I said, "Send him a text message and tell him how you feel," well, you probably thought of that already too and you've already talked yourself out of it because right after you send the message you'd feel dumb and cheap." *

"Dumb, yes," Angel replies, "but cheap? I don't know." *

"My point is," Scrounge continues, "the way you're feeling right now; I been there. Believe me, and I know all too well about the deep hurt that a love lost can inflict." Scrounge looks questioningly back at Angel and says, "For me, knowing there's no turning back time and probably no turning this thing around, I say, Move on." *

"I think I get it, mom." Angel says knowingly. "I think you're right. *

Scrounge steps out of the tent gently pulling Angel out with her. Music begins for, **'When Love Doesn't Take Off'**

51

When Love Doesn't Take Off

Angel takes the note from her pocket and reads it a second time, and looking rather despondent, she sings,

> When love doesn't take off
> there's no words can amply say,
> what it is, how it feels, what do you do
> when there's just no running away.

Angel glances at her mother, turns away and looks out into the audience and sings,...

> Been standing here for a while staring into space
> like there's something odd
> about being the one left behind
> kind of like,... when love doesn't take off.

Scrounge steps over to stand next to Angel, glances at Angel before turning to face the audience and Scrounge sings,

> *When love doesn't take off*
> *there's no place to hide away,*
> and it seems like everybody knows,
> as they watch you go your way.

Scrounge almost looks angry as she sings,

> And it's seems they want me to fail;
> fall in line with the unfortunate lot,
> I guess it's fun to watch someone going down in flames
> like,... when love doesn't take off.

Angel raises her arms and hands out questioningly before she's joined by Scrounge and together, they sing,

> When love doesn't take off
> there's always a hope for tomorrow's scene
> but in the end, what matters most;
> all I ask for is some dignity.

Scrounge steps away, Angel steps forward, resigned to her star-crossed situation, she grins wryly and sings,

> Cause when love doesn't take off,
> or for someone to win, somebody's got to lose
> and the odds are in my favor,
> sooner or later, I'm gonna get the news.

Scrounge steps forward, standing next to Angel, Scrounge puts her arm around her daughter as she sings,

> If things start to turn, I'm just gonna say,
> "I have to go to bed; I got a bad cough"
> and like me they can take it or leave it,
> doesn't matter when love doesn't take off.

Angel and Scrounge sing together,

> When love doesn't take off,

As Scrounge stands singing the end of the song,

> Yeah; yeah, when love doesn't take off

Angel picks up the 'Guitar with No Strings' and begins playing it like she knows what she's doing; glancing over at her mother, Angel sees Scrounges' face smiling agreeably and Angel smiles back with mutual admiration as she plays the 'Guitar with No Strings' until the end of the song

52

ACT TWO - SCENE ELEVEN

ACT TWO — SCENE ELEVEN:

The Players:
FAITH, HOOT, SCROUNGE, ANGEL,
GLADSTONE, PRINCESS & BOBBY

EXT. THE TENT CIRCLE: "Looks like it's starting to get light, Hoot." Faith says, as they both sit on a folded sleeping bag, huddled close to each other in front of their tent; her head is resting on Hoot's shoulder and they have a shared wool army blanket wrapped around them. "It'll be happening soon enough." Faith continues, as she snuggles even closer to Hoot. "We should get up and start putting our things together." *

"No," Hoot replies softly as he continues to look out and survey the surroundings, "There'll be time enough for the big push and all that other stuff later. We'll only have two block to go; it won't take that much time and I was just feeling; you know, the last night in, 'the Circle,' us being here in each other's arms, surrounded by our friends;" Hoot looks down to Faith and gently kisses the top of her head. He looks up and away again. He breathes heavily in and out, and says, almost whispering, "I just want to kind of keep this moment for a little while longer, okay?" *

After a long silent pause, Faith says, "Hoot, I'm kind of worried." She takes her head off from his shoulder and, looking up at him as he continues to look out and she asks, "Are we gonna be okay? I mean, I know we'll continue to be blessed by the Lord,... He's carried us so far, but Hoot," Faith reaches up to Hoot's head and gently turns Hoot's face down so he is looking into her face. As Faith looks back, her countenance washed in apprehension, she says, "Hoot, we've been through a lot, but we've never faced this kind of adversity before and,..." Concerned, Faith looks up and says, "You know I can't help but be worried about this." *

"Faith," Hoot answers, "We talked about this,..." Hoot breathes in heavily and continues, "We talked about this a whole lot. We got somewhere to go for now." *

"I know, I know." Faith returns. "But today I'm worried again." *

Hoot laughs and says, "Oh Faith; ye of little,..." Hoot laughs. "Faith, we got this." Hoot says, squeezing her in closely. "Something's gonna come up; always does." *

"Hoot, I'm being serious here." Faith presses. "Look where we are; look what's happened to us?" *

"We are not down and out," Hoot answers. "Look, we're,… we are going forward, just not as fast as we'd like. We got enough in savings to have that, 'Sidewalk organization' get us into an apartment, but we'll never get back into a house—not with us as old as we are unless we keep saving. And we're not a good credit risk; we got zip for collateral; the Bank of America, who are ultimately responsible for what's happened to us,… they're not gonna loan us money for a house,… not on such a paltry fixed income,…" Hoot looks over knowingly and continues, "Not that I'd ever even think about using the Bank of America again, but I been talking to Bob at the WSECU credit union, and with them,… if we come up with a big down payment, we can make it happen. We just gotta hold on for another couple months." *

"You make me smile." Faith says smiling. "You make it sound so possible even though you and I both know it's not that easy. It's never that easy. And this, "another couple months" thing has been our mantra for over a year. But I do like your optimism,…" She looks back expectantly and asks, "but are we good?" *

Hoot stands up, reaches out his hand for Faith's hand and pulls her up to a standing position. As Hoot steps in close, Faith looks apprehensive. Hoot pulls her in even closer, embracing her and asks, "May I have this dance?" *

Faith at first is hesitant but seconds later as the music plays and Hoot pulls Faith in even closer, embracing her and Faith smiles effervescently as she looks into Hoot's eyes,… She is acceptingly composed and happy. Hoot starts to dance; a slow, close dance as Hoot looks deeply into her eyes.

At first, they dance within the small and cluttered confines of,

'the Circle,' until Hoot, steps them off the curb and he begins to serenade Faith as they romantically dance in the deserted street, Hoot is looking into Faith's eyes lovingly, smiling at times, both of them having a hard time holding back their emotions, and all the while, holding close to each other, Hoot and Faith begins to sing,...
'What We've Done With Our Lives'

53

What We've Done With Our Lives

Hoot sings the first few lines of the song;

> I remember the day when our new world began
> seeing you for the first time on the other side

Faith looks back knowingly and sings;

> and us sharing our fries at break while working at Burger Chef
> both searching for what is life.

Hoot softly reminds Faith of their early days as he sings;

> and I remember pushing my bike alongside of us
> as we navigated through downtown Portland in seventy-two

Faith looks back knowingly as she replies with a smile;

    and the touch of your hand safely in mine as we walked
    in the evening rain, on our way down Park Avenue

*The pace of the dance seems to slow a bit as Hoot's face turns serious
as he sings;*

    I remember praying for you to be the one
    to end my loneliness and bring me round right

Faith's eyes beam brightly with wonder as she sings;

    and with our very same hopes and prayers,
    you came to me to share so far

The both seem to embrace even tighter as they both sing in harmony;

    with what we've done with our lives

*Hoot seems to lose step and cadence with the dance before he corrects
himself and turning to Faith, Hoot sings;*

    I remember the helpless feelings that we both bore
    and the tearful sorry streaming from your eyes

*As if she was reading his thoughts, Faith looks back with concerned
sorrow as she sings;*

    that day when everything stood so silently still
    after losing one of the stars of the show; our prize

Hoot looks away in thought before he looks concerned but then relaxes after regaining his composure and he sings softly;

> Yeah, and I remember
> just how brave and courageous you were
> steering us away from sirens of hopelessness,

And now it's Faith's turn to move forward in time and emotions as she sings;

> yeah and I remember a special gift of tender mercies
> with another child to have, to love; to bless.

Hoot smiles congenially as he looks into Faith's face and sings;

> And I remember us as a team working to raise a family
> pressing forward; ever on to new heights

And now Faith, feeling the message of the song, rather excitedly inter-jects her thoughts to Hoot as she sings;

> but to see how we've grown from then to now,
> I'm so happy with

Hoot and Faith seem to twirl in a few circles as they both sing in harmony;

> what we've done with our lives

At this point there is an intermezzo of music that encourages the both of them to freely dance across the street in soft circling motion, almost touching the curb at the other side of the street before they return to the

*center of the street dancing on the dividing lines,... and this time, Faith
begins to sing the new verse;*

> I remember the day when our last child flew off;
> oh, how brave and strong you pretended to be back then
> and I remember how we spent those many days and nights
> getting to know a little bit more about each other again

Now it's Hoot's turn to reply in verse as he sings;

> And I remember just how daring and fearless we were
> braving all the new adventures that you kept thinking of,
> and now I see your smile;
> your eyes burning brightly back at me
> saying I'm so glad to have you to love.

Faith looks back into Hoot's loving eyes and smiles as she sings;

> I see us as eternal, moving forward, doing good
> and I see you and I in the middle of the rise

*Hoot and Faith seem to sway a bit as they both sing the last verses
together;*

> we've come so far and loved so much;
> hard not to be amazed
> with what we've done with our lives,...
> what we've done with our lives; yeah,...

*When Faith and Hoot finish singing the words to the song they get even
closer and they continue dancing until the music fades away,... and then
they stop and kiss,...*

54

⚜

ACT TWO - SCENE TWELVE

ACT TWO — SCENE TWELVE:

The Players:
HOOT, FAITH, JEROME, SCROUNGE, ANGEL,
GLADSTONE, PRINCESS, PRIVATE & BOBBY,

EXT. THE TENT CIRCLE: Police begin to arriving in pairs from outside the four corners of the mitigation site, going through camp shaking tents and ordering them to get up and start their process of moving out. *

One of the two officers walking down from State Street approaches Hoot and Faith. "Do you two live here?" The policeman asks, pointing to the mitigation site. *

Faith shyly nods. *

259

"You need to get out of the street." The officer declares. *

"Yeah, you're probably right." Hoot says proudly as he grabs Faith's hand and walks to the curb. *

"Well, you need to get your stuff together and you need to be off this site by nine o'clock." The officer announces, "Or you'll forfeit all your belongings and they'll end up going," He points to a loud truck that is offloading a large trash receptacle on the sidewalk on State Street, "in one of those dumpsters over there." *

As the officer is walking away, Jerome calls out, "Hey, can I ask you a couple questions?" *

"Son," The officer replies with a calm demeanor, "I can tell you, we had nothing to do with telling folks they could stay if they cleaned up this place. I'm sorry, but you need to get your things outta here, right now." The officer says as he walks away, "So if you'll excuse me," he points to the back of the lot, "I need to get back with my partner over there." *

Jerome walks along with the officer. "No, I didn't want to talk about that. I didn't really believe that scuttlebutt. I knew they just wanted us to clean up our mess." *

The officer stops for a moment, turns and says irately, "You're right; it's your mess. And now you're costing the taxpayers a lot more money and time and labor to clean it all up." *

As Jerome calmly listens, he nods acceptingly with a grin before walking back to, 'the Circle.'. *

"What was that all about?" Scrounge questions turning for a second to look at Jerome. *

"I was talking to that cop," Jerome answers, "And almost implicated myself as an accessory to a crime." *

"That doesn't sound like the Jerome I know." Scrounge says looking at Jerome. *

"I was so caught up in trying to find out about what happened to Private," Jerome replies, "That I almost implicated myself into a self-incrimination. And as you may know, fleeing from the scene of a crime can be a criminal offense in and of itself." Jerome sorts through his backpack and continues, "And if that guy wasn't such a jerk about it, I might have been stupid enough to tell myself out." Jerome pauses and says, "It's so hard to pander to bureaucracy and the weaknesses of our beloved incompetent city administration, what with their lack of flexibility and initiative, combined with excessive adherence to regulations; so marked by officialism, red tape, and proliferation." *

"Now that's the Jerome I know." Scrounge laughingly replies. *

As Hoot walks back to the tent with Faith he says, "Looks like it's time for the big push; we better wake up the sleeping Princess." He smiles at Faith and says, "Thank you for the dance." *

"I'm awake." Princess declares, stepping out of the tent. "I been awake for hours." She smiles, looking down shyly before looking back up and saying with a guilty grin, "I was peeking through an opening in the tent and I watched you two dancing in the streets." *

"Dancing in the streets." Hoot replies. "That could be a good hook for a song." *

Faith hugs Princess before stepping in the tent. "Hey, Hoot." Faith says peeking out of the tent, "Looks like we had a little elf surprise us getting our gear ready while we all slept last night." *

"Yeah," Princess replies, noticing Gladstone is looking over at her, "Surprised me too." *

"If you might remember," Hoot replies, "We didn't really get to sleep last night." *

"Well, thank you, honey." Faith says coming out and giving Princess another hug. *

Princess steps over to Bobby's area to find that Bobby has already packed up most of her belongings, has put things into a neat pile but hasn't dismantled and folded up her tent. You need any help?" Princess asks. *

"Some folks that have been accepted to be able to go over there," Bobby says, sitting down on her duffle bag, pointing to the new mitigation site a block away, "are just leaving all their stuff here. They'll be moving into a new tent over there anyway; provided by the city." Bobby surveys her surroundings, seeing growing piles of trash and junk forming with scattered rubbish and debris in piles everywhere. "I was kind of hoping that that pipe dream last night was really going to happen." She looks over at Private's tent before saying, "Should a known, city ain't that kind." *

"Or honest." Princess replies. *

Bobby looks away and says, "For me, this was all kind a good while it lasted." *

As Gladstone carries out two boxes and a couple garbage bags containing his possessions and puts them in a large fold-out canvas wagon, Princess asks, "Do you need any help?" *

"I'm just about done." Gladstone answers. "I didn't sleep at all last night either." Gladstone steps up close to Princess and takes one of her hands. "But thank you for asking." He looks into her face and is again captivated by her beautiful blue eyes. "I don't know what your plans are," Gladstone says without losing eye contact, "But like Hoot, I believe that the universe is entrusting me to take care of you." *

"You and Hoot were talking about me?" Princess asks. "Why should you guys care? I mean, we've only known each other for a couple days?" *

"Sometimes," Gladstone remarks, "things happen because they were meant to." He smiles and says, "Maybe the universe has put us together knowing we are both alone in this world; that we need each other and maybe we were supposed to help each other to get through these uncertain times." *

"By universe," Princess asks, warmly, "You mean God?" *

Gladstone hesitates before answering. "In that song that I sang you last night?" He questions, "I said we need to be honest with each other to get by." Gladstone looks off for a second at the tent compound that is being haphazardly dismantled before turning back to

Princess, and says, "I don't admit this to other people, not even to Hoot and Faith, but, I don't know, I do believe that life, or the universe, cannot have arisen by chance; meaning that it had to have been designed and created by some intelligent entity." Gladstone looks down as he says, "I don't know all that church stuff. I don't know anything with any sureness." He looks back up at Princess and says, "But I believe there's something out there; I just don't have all the information yet." He looks into Princess's eyes and says, "And I believe there's something here between me and you; I just don't have all the information yet." *

Princess looks thoughtful as she replies, "I,.. I feel something between us too." She smiles and says softly, "I just don't have all the information yet." *

Their laughter is interrupted as Bobby says, "This is all very touching, but," Bobby points to the rest of the encampment with the whole mitigation site in disarray as people are lethargically on the move with their belongings, in spite of being rushed by the prodding of the police, or the threateningly loud growling of the backhoe engines, already turned on, being revving up in the back parts of the parking lot of the encampment. "We need to get outta here, right?" *

Gladstone turns to Bobby with a serious look and says, "I'm not really feeling this, but,..." He waves a finger over at Private's tent. "Should we be taking care of his stuff?" *

"Not me." Bobby replies turning away from Gladstone. "Too personal." Bobby pulls out a traveling bag with wheels from her tent and sets it next to the duffle bag. "Anyway," She continues, "What would we do with his stuff anyway?" She pauses sadly, breathes in slowly before saying, "Do you want his things?" *

"No," Gladstone answers. "I got more than I can handle getting all my stuff in this wagon." *

Seeing Bobby disassembling her now empty tent, Princess goes over to help. "Thank you." Bobby says. "Could you get on that corner over there?" Bobby asks, pointing without looking away from her work. You'll need to peal that duct tape off." *

"Got it." Princess replies, amiably. *

"I think it best," Bobby says to Gladstone, "we have the city tractors scoop up his stuff and throw it away." *

"You mean you don't even want to see what's in there?" A voice calls from behind Bobby. *

"Private!" Bobby yells, running to him and throwing her arms around Private's shoulders. "Jerome said you got shot." She cries. Suddenly she is fraught with anger and she breaks free of the embrace and punches Private's shoulder as she cries out, "We all thought you were dead." *

"As Mark Twain said," Private remarks with a smile, "The reports of my death are greatly exaggerated." *

Private is joined be Hoot, Faith, Gladstone, Princess and Angel. "Just like old times." Private says smiling. *

"Private!" Jerome yells from across the street as he runs up. "We all thought you were,..." *

"Yeah, yeah." Private replies, "Everybody thought I was dead." *

"But I saw you go down," Jerome says, "when Roger shot you." *

Private looks at Jerome with a note of annoyance on his face. "Yeah," Private replies, "I went down. And I tried to get you to go down too,... but you just stood there like an idiot, and then Roger shot again and you bolted." *

"You saw me running away?" Jerome asks with incredulity. *

Private laughs. "Watching you running through the garbage in the dark was so comical, man." *

"But you got shot." Jerome says, "I watched you go down." Jerome pointing to Private's m65 army field jacket and says, "I see all this blood,..." Jerome looks concerned and asks, "Where'd you get shot?" *

"When this all happened, and I saw the flash of his gun, I instinctively ducked for cover, and seeing's as how there wasn't any cover, I fell to the ground. And like I said, I grabbed at you on my way down for you to get to safety too. But it all happened so fast. I'm really glad you got away, man." *

Jerome looks ashamed as he says, "but I ditched you and,..." *

Private puts his arm tightly around Jerome's shoulders and shakes him as he says, "But you're still alive, man. I'm really happy. And I'm proud of how you tried to come to my aid." Private comically shakes Jerome one more time before releasing him and says with a serious tone, "This ain't my blood, "It's Dumpster's." *

With everybody suddenly in shock, instinctively each one looks LL around the area for Dumpster. *

Bobby asks with A renewed sense of concern, "So what happened to Dumpster? Is he,... dead?" *

"No." Answers Private encouragingly. "He's gonna be okay." *

"What happened to him?" Bobby repeats. *

"So, when Roger took his first shot," Private answers, "and I'm still not sure who or what Roger's target was, I dropped down to the ground. Dumpster took off like a bolt of lightning; I think he was gonna put the hurt on Roger, but I was still holding his leash and when the dog got to the end of it, the force nearly pulled my arm out from its socket. It still hurts." *

"So," Jerome says slyly, "you had a hold of him all the time." *

Private rubs his shoulder and says, "Anyway, I'm there holding him back and then Roger shoots him. And I'm still not sure that that was what Roger intended to do, I mean, it was dark and he was still high on something; I kind a think he was aiming at you, Jerome and then accidently shot my dog instead. Shot him in his right shoulder above his leg and the impact knocked him out. And I thought he *was* dead." *

"Oh," Bobby says sympathetically as she begins to cry, "Poor Dumpster." *

"Bobby," Private says understandingly, "He's gonna be okay." Private looks determined as he says, "When I saw he got hit with the second bullet, and Jerome had taken off, I pulled on the leash and pulled Dumpster's limp body back to me and found he was still alive. I was really mad, but I knew Dumpster needed help, so I picked him up; and let me tell you, he's a heavy dog, and now I got this bad shoulder, but I picked him up and carried him to the 'Oly Vet's' over on Union; They already knew Dumpster and me, and lucky for us both, they're open twenty-four hours. They fixed him up, and he's spending the night at their kennel." *

"That's really good news." Faith responds as she gingerly hugs Private. "I'm glad you're okay." *

"And," Private continues looking directly at Bobby, "I thought maybe you'd like to go with me to pick him up later on this morning." *

Bobby's eyes shine as she says, "I'd love that." *

"Meanwhile," Private reports, "Time for us to finish packing and get out of here." *

It's early morning, March 5th 2019. A fresh group of police have arrived and in pairs, they continue the big project push of evacuating everybody from the mitigation site on State Street. Their mission is to have the lot cleared by noon and they don't care where the vagrants go, just that they do go away. *

"They'll soon be back, and in greater numbers." Hoot remarks, looking all around. "It's 7:30, and probably 20 percent of our neighbors have already evacuated their spaces." *

Faith, stares out and says, "Looks like some of em," She points in different directions, "David over there, and Winston over there; they just left their tents and stuff and their pallets behind." She looks at Hoot and says, "As well as all their garbage. And look at all the debris in the spaces where their tents were." *

"Destitution and hopelessness will do that to people." Hoot replies. "It all comes down to them blaming us for the situation we're in here. But,... it's gonna be a long day, so let's keep a little optimistic here,...." *

Jerome steps over and interjects, "My favorite of all of this circus spectacle is the city bringing in all those backhoes with their engines idling loudly in the back of the encampment; giving everyone an early-morning wakeup call, and a hurry-up reminder to all the homeless here that the City of Olympia means business." *

"Well," Hoot replies, "they wanted us gone by 9:00 but as you can see, that ain't gonna happen, even with all those large dumpsters that were trucked in over there on State Street." Hoot tips his hat forward as he scratches the back of his head and says, "But the city is really ready and wanting to get rid of us as soon as possible." *

"If you define yourself by the power to take life," Jerome spouts, "the desire to dominate, to possess...then you have nothing." *

Faith turns to Jerome and asks, "So where are you headed? Do you have some place to go?" *

Jerome points to the back corner of the encampment and says, "Looks like the city's got backup. There's more trucks waiting back there." Jerome looks in another direction as he replies, "I was planning on going with Private, but it looks like he's in love and, I'm happy for him and Bobby, but..." Jerome turns and looks out at the compound as he says, "Looks like everyone is up." *

"It's odd," Hoot replies, "Seeing these people, uh, neighbors and friends out there collecting their things; some are putting em in piles and taking their tents apart, and some are just staying in their tents, kind a like they can't believe it's all happening." *

"I think some of them are just waiting for the last minute," Jerome responds, smiling wryly, "I like to think that they're daring the city administration and the cops to make the next move." *

"Seeing those guys walking their stuff to the new mitigation site," Faith replies as she points to a small group of straggled people dragging plastic bags and carrying cardboard boxes across or into the street, "kind of like Exodus without Moses. Doomed to forever wander but without leadership or guidance." *

"Pretty bleak picture you're painting there, Hon." Hoot replies. "But some of them folk heading to the new 'Coopersville' Hoot looks knowingly at Faith as he says, "But they have a small idea or plan on how to get out of here.". *

"But so many don't." Faith replies with sadness on her face. "And they're just dealing with circumstances beyond their control." *

"What saddens me," Jerome replies, "Is seeing all those others, standing around in disbelief, refusing to accept the fact that the city would actually evict them from here." He smiles. "And that lawyer trying to help us? Spencer I think,... he's doing his best, but it doesn't matter how many laws are broken here by the city, Spencer won't be able to stop this anymore." *

Scrounge ties a knot to secure a box and says to Angel, "There's a lot of anger out here ready to explode." *

"Well can you blame them?" Faith replies irritably. "They got no place to go and they can't believe that the city, that the people of Olympia, would forsake them in their time of need." *

"But," Hoot says pointing to the street, "In answer to their sad plight, as they are being driven out, there's people from all over the area,..." Hoot points to a truck pulled up next to the curb, "They're loading Victor's stuff right there." Hoot turns to Faith and says, "Bureaucracy may have its, 'bean counters' and, 'wishful thinking city council persons' but never doubt the goodness of the human spirit." *

They look out at the new sea of volunteers that have shown up to lend a hand; some with shovels and rakes and garbage bags, some with wheelbarrows, others with their own personal trucks to help the expelled and dispossessed be able to collect what things they can, to move them to their new locations. *

"All packed up with nowhere to go." Scrounge reports smiling as she and Angel join Hoot, Faith and Jerome. "Well, it was real good while it lasted." *

"Speak for yourself." Angel chimes in. "This hasn't been the best place we've ever been to." *

"Sorry about that Angel." Scrounge replies reticently. "I haven't been at the top of my game for a while. But I'm on it now, and we're gonna get to a better place; I promise." *

Scrounge smiles at Angel as she points to her phone and lifts up one eyebrow and says, "She called. They're on their way to pick us up. We'll be heading for Cle Elum in Eastern Washington for a while if that's okay with you." *

"What?" Angel exclaims excitedly. "No way!" *

"That's wonderful." Says Bobby as she gives Scrounge a hug. *

"You can't win, Vader." Gladstone says as he steps up holding hands with Princess, "If you strike me down, I shall become more powerful than you can possibly imagine." *

"This is our most desperate hour." Princess reports. "Help me, Obi-Wan Kenobi. You're my only hope." *
"Good to have you lighten things up here." Hoot replies. *

"You know," Gladstone says, smiling. "Sometimes I amaze even myself." *

"The truth is often what we make of it." Hoot counters. "And I see you've corrupted Princess here." *

"What I think is funny," Gladstone says, changing the subject, "In spite of the city's deadline, most of these guys are still not getting their stuff together. And in all this chaos and confusion there's some still in denial, walking around aimlessly, maybe thinking things will go away." *

"How about the police over there," Bobby replies, pointing with a nod of her head, "He's shaking tents, getting people up and out. It's gotta be hard on the weaker ones." *

"How about that?" Private spouts, standing behind Bobby. "Those guys are fighting over almost worthless possessions; that old holey blanket? That tarp with the rip in it? You'd think the sounds of those tractors scraping the parking lot over there would bring them down to earth." *

"If they're not careful," Gladstone interjects with narrowed eyes, " they're gonna get collected like everything in their path and get dumped into one of those dumpsters over there." *

"Speaking about Dumpster," Bobby declares, "When do we get him back?" *

"On our way out." Private answers. "If he's ready." *

"Where is out to?" Faith questions. "Do you have some place to land?" *

"We're not too sure, just yet." Private replies, looking at Bobby. "But we're going it together." *

"That's nice." Faith replies. "Two can make it better than one." *

"Two?" Bobby replies. "Dumpster's coming with us too." She pauses and continues, "Oh, and Jerome." *

"I am?" Jerome asks disbelievingly, seeing Private and Bobby looking at him as if to say, "Well, duh!" *

"When all of this is done," Princess replies, "I hope the city is happy; but I got a feeling they won't be,... and in a year or so I'm thinking they'll be ready to dismantle the new mitigation site and make trouble all over again." *

"Trouble." Hoot replies. "We got us trouble." *

And amidst all of this, the finale music begins for; **'Resilient, (Rise & Shine)'**

55

R E S I L I E N T - (Rise And Shine)

— FINALE NUMBER —

RESILIENT (RISE AND SHINE)

The Players:
HOOT, FAITH, JEROME, SCROUNGE, ANGEL, PRIVATE, BOBBY, PRINCESS & GLADSTONE

HOOT packing up his belongings, looks up and sings;

Trouble, trouble, oh, trouble, we got us trouble
Trouble that holds us back from what we could be;
Trouble that prevents us from breaking free
Trouble, yeah, trouble

FAITH looks up to the heavens as she sings,

Trouble, trouble,
Trouble how we're thought of to be lesser than;\
Trouble that hurts us over and over again
Oh, trouble, yeah, trouble

With a look of contemplation, **JEROME** *stands to the side of everyone as he sings,*

Trouble, Trouble
Trouble that chooses who gets on the bus;
Trouble that doesn't care what happens to us
Hey, hey, trouble; we got us trouble

And as she's holding hands with her mother, **ANGEL** *sings,*

But we can't let hate and despair tell us out;
We need to have love define what we're about
Yeah, to get us going on our way
to the path that leads us out

And now, **EVERYONE** *seems to look out at the faces of different people in the audience, they all sing out in harmony,*

Rise and shine;
Taking in the new sun's healing rays
Rise and shine;
With remarkable hopes for better days
There's a new life to plan and architect,
to build to our own design

HOOT — Oh, we are brave,

FAITH — we are strong,

JEROME — We are resilient

EVERYONE — We rise and shine;
Rise and shine

BOBBY, *looks around the compound that looks like the aftermath of a war zone and glancing at PRIVATE before she sings,*

Trouble, trouble; trouble, we got us trouble
Trouble that amplifies our mistrust and fear;
trouble that holds us ever captive here
Yeah, trouble; mm, trouble

PRIVATE *smiles back at Bobby before turning to the audience and with a sad grin, he sings,*

Trouble, trouble
Trouble bound in meddlesome red tape;
trouble that screams out, "No there is no escape."
Hey, hey, hey, trouble, Oh, trouble

PRINCESS *looks out at the audience as if she's expecting them to sing, but when they don't, she sings,*

Trouble, trouble
Trouble that confines us to where we live;
trouble that won't forget and won't forgive
Oh, trouble, we got us trouble

GLADSTONE steps up behind PRINCESS and puts his hands on her shoulders as he sings,

But there's a beacon glowing outside the wasteland
as good folks see our plight and take a stand
Oh, to offer kindnesses and care
with love and a helping hand

*And once again, **EVERYONE** looks out at and into the many faces of the different people in the audience, and they all sing out in harmony,*

Rise and shine;
taking in the new sun's healing rays
Rise and shine;
with remarkable hopes for better days
There's a new life for us to architect
and build to our very own design

BOBBY — Oh, we are brave,

PRIVATE — we are strong;

PRINCESS — we are resilient,

GLADSTONE — Oh, resilient

EVERYONE — And we rise and shine
Rise and shine

56

END of, 'R E S I L I E N T'
- The Musical Play & Story

BY

LORD CHESTER L. BALDWIN II

END OF ACT TWO OF

'RESILIENT'

AN EPOSODIC, WEB-BASED

MUSICAL PLAY & STORY

57

— ABOUT THE AUTHOR —

LORD CHESTER L. BALDWIN II, OR SIMPLY PUT; Lord Baldwin,... is a Writer, Musician, Songwriter, Graphic Artist and now, Playwright, as well as a Singer-Performer that lives in the Pacific Northwest. Lord Baldwin is happily married and has ten children.

IN 1967 LORD BALDWIN ATTENDED GLENDORA HIGH SCHOOL, and began his writing career writing short stories and poetry. It was at that time that his English teacher, Miss Ohlrich, impressed with his work, entered some of Lord Baldwin's works to a national forum competition,... but he never found out the results because his mother, a sad victim of repeated domestic violence, ran away and took the kids with her by train to the East Coast and landed in New York City.

IN 1968 AFTER HAVING MOVED TO BROWNS MILLS NEW JERSEY, and while going to, Pemberton Township High School, Lord Baldwin continued to write poetry (Lyrics) and short stories which also caught the attention of his English teacher, (sorry can't remember their name), who encouraged him to share his works with another competition in New York City, but Lord Baldwin had turned his attention and energies to writing lyrics to songs. It was also here in New Jersey that he composed and recorded his musical composition, 'Rain.'

AND BLA BLA BLA,... you know the truth is, if you're reading this to find out my credentials,... well, this is the first time I've ever written and published a musical play,... so, no experience,... and as you can see by the end product, I didn't quite follow the rules,... having everybody's name capitalized just looked, I don't know, un-appealing to look at and uninviting to read,... and no, I don't see it as a rock opera,... more I think as a story about the plight of some Americans that have fallen down on their resources,...

AND ABOUT THE SONGS?,... What's going on there?,... What kind of music is it anyway? To be fair to you, I have never, from over the fifty years of songwriting and recording,... I have never found the right label for what I do with music and song,... sure there's a lot of blues involved, and hey, a huge part of my life's repertoire is steeped in the blues,... but I do not follow the primary harmonic structure of the blues which was derived from church music of the South; you know, the, 'I-IV-V' progression,... first, I feel guilty re-peating myself when I can colour the story that much better with a few more good words,... secondly, I got this music thing in my head that says, "that'll sound a lot better with a graced minor chord here and there,... and my harmonica has kept me involved with the blues,... but there's so much more,... me and rock and roll grew up together and we know each other pretty well,...

I KNEW WHEN I STARTED MY JOURNEY that I would never be a quality guitar player,... oh, I put in my time and I'm okay, but to be great you need to have a commitment to put all your energies into that one thing,... I had a love for the writing the verses and composing the music for the completion of the song itself more,... that's where my heart was and still is,... which took priority over all the extended time commitments to practicing,... and after I'd finished writing a poem and I would try to feel out what the mood of the music could be,... I'd get really excited to see what key I was gonna do the song in and with and what chords I would be using to accompany the words,...

I LIKE TO THINK that my music is a different kind of Jazz,... giving me the freedom to take my music anywhere it calls or leads me to,... and so I would practice the chords and the progressions for that one song until I had it saved to memory and I would move on to the next poem and the next arrangement, leaving no time to get better on the guitar or for that matter, the keyboards,...

AND I LOVE RHYTHUM & BLUES and soul music,... so when someone asks me what genre or kind of music it is that I do,... I eventually resort to making myself rather unrelatable when I answer, "Jazz." And I find that some people do listen to Jazz,...

BUT ME A PLAYWRIGHT,...? I don't know, I have written a few books,... I have written hundreds of poems to lyrics over the years,... and so, why not? An arguable truth here is that I am driven to do this thing,... and I forgave myself a long time ago for not being better on lead guitar, especially if there was another song coming out to meet me,... maybe in a dream, or maybe it was a ditty that popped in my head on my way to work; a new song being born as I'm driving down the road,... I think the thing I want to report is, if you are a story teller and you write poetry or lyrics for songs, hey, this web-based format gives you a lot more latitude to say the story and sing the songs than the conventional Broadway play,... and it may not seem like it, but I read and reread and try to say things with the least amount of words,... I really do fight for brevity,... honest I do,... but then you get caught up within the story and as the characters come to life you just know each one is gonna want to say a lot more than you want them to,... and there's nine characters, taken directly out of my experiences working for 'Sidewalk' and many of the lyrics came out of our clients' experiences,...

AND **I WAS THERE** THAT ,...

IT WAS AN EARLY TUESDAY MORNING, March 5th 2019 when I got a call from my son, Spencer, who informed me that the houseless people in the tent occupation on State Street and Franklin were being evicted,... and **I was there** when the tractors screamed into that cold morning,... and I saw desperation in some, but to many others there was this spirit of accomplishment,... they had to move on, but there was a, 'Spirit of Resilience' that said that they'd be okay,... and the fact that they had been part of a thing bigger than themselves or even the Olympia City Hall,... and it was their own, 'Badge of Courage' worn as they were leaving,... and they were survivors of the system that was overwhelmed by the overall systemic homeless problem that is worldwide,... And I really wanted to be able to document the essence of what went on prior that fateful day,... to give voice to the silenced ones that were pushed out of sight and mind,... feeling the hard times in play as they were getting pushed out of the way,... and mostly nobody noticing,... hey, times had gotten kind a tough,... as others and outsiders guiltily look the other way,... but, *"how many times can a man turn his head and pretend that he just doesn't see?"*,...

I FELT I COULD DO THIS; that I could give voice to this sad happening,... so I wrote this play,... created this story,... accompanied by these songs,... and it ended up being what it is,...

IT MAY INTEREST YOU TO KNOW,... this book could have had three or four other numbers included in it, and maybe in the future we could consider it, but for now, I felt like the important parts of the story for the most part had been dutifully addressed or satisfied so I ended it,... but just for the record, I considered the song, **'Everybody Falls Down'** taken from the, *'Nevertheless,..'* album,... Sung by Private to Bobby to bolster her anxieties and give her hope for the future and solidify how Private feels about her,... and from the album, *'World On Fire'* is a song, **'We Can Forgive'** sung by Princess, (you may have noticed that she didn't get to have a cameo song), but I felt from her outsider perspective and her extreme empathy for others, I envisioned Princess singing to the group as they are buffeted by the bureaucracy of the system and their seemingly uncaring city,... maybe sung at the close of ACT ONE to again, leave a lingering sense of hope,... Thirdly, from the album, *'When The World Opens Up Again'* there were two songs for consideration,... the first, called, **'Hooverville'** that is all about the mentality of being down and out and trapped in the never-ending cycle of being pushed around because you're poor,... I had Scrounge in mind to sing this one,... amplifying her anxiety of going nowhere fast,... or, **'Weighted Down'** also sung as a duet by Scrounge and Jerome who share the verses, and sung around the beginning of, 'ACT TWO' to add a sense of how uncomfortable it is to be homeless in such unpredictable times,..., and there were other songs I briefly considered but let it go for the sake of,... are you ready?,... for the sake of *brevity*,...

MANY ASPIRE TO DO GREAT THINGS, especially when they recognize that they've been entrusted with particular talents and gifts,... It takes time and soul searching to discover the potential of those gifts,... but even from the beginning of the process, some will begin to sculpture and to feed and to modify and to nurture their special dreams,... that they might grow into that distinct singular vision of that dream,... where one day, they will be able to **Shine**,... and be able to bask in their own bright **Starlight**.